B-SIDES AND REMIXES

A NOVEL

RAN WALKER

B-SIDES AND REMIXES

Images used courtesy of Pixabay.com.

ISBN: 9781020001048

45 Alternate Press, LLC
Hampton, VA

For Elle

SIDE A

1

———

"**P**age forty-nine," J says. He tosses the magazine on the counter, barely able to hide his smile, then grabs the stool next to mine.

"What are you talking about?" I ask. I stare at the beautiful black model on the cover. "*Soul Sista*? Dude, you know this is a women's magazine, right?"

"Page forty-nine," J repeats.

Opening the magazine, I laugh when I see a picture of myself at the front of the eligible bachelor feature. I had agreed to do this so long ago that it had slipped my mind. In the amount of time it took for them to actually run the issue, I could have long since met Miss Right—not that I had, but I just could have.

"Cool, this is exactly what we needed, man. Maybe now we can get the word out about this place on a national level," J says, hovering over me while I scan the profile.

That was our hope, assuming the profile ever ran. We were barely getting by, and if things didn't pick up soon, we would probably have to explore our exit options—not that we didn't plan to go out swinging like Ken Griffey, Jr., though.

When I see the words "co-founder of C&J's Rare Grooves, Harlem" beneath my picture, I smile. In the grand scope of things, this is a relatively small coup, but with our micro-budget for advertising, publicity is better than any ad we could run.

"Look here," I say to J, pointing at the page. "Out of all the stuff I answered in the profile, this is all they printed: 'My dream woman would embody the lyrics of a Stevie Wonder song.'"

J nods. "Yo, that's hot."

"Dude, I said a lot more than that, but they trimmed most of it out."

"Come on, Cool. It's like twenty-something other guys in this section. They couldn't make you the only brotha on the list. Trust me. You still get to be 'the man' for a month. Don't sweat it. They just better be glad they didn't put my ass up in that piece."

I chuckle. "J, you might've been too direct."

"I definitely wouldn't have said that smooth shit you said. I would've been like, 'Just hook a brother up with YaYa Da Costa and I'm straight.'"

"Where's the poetry in that?" I offer.

"I'll leave the poetry to Hill Harper-looking ne-groes like you."

"I'm taller, dude."

"Not from where I stand," J laughs, while ex-tending his six foot four inch frame.

Scanning the bachelor section, I see all kinds of brothas: the dressed-to-impress brotha, the Morris Chestnut-type brotha, the Christopher Williams-type brother, a Wesley or two, a rookie pro athlete, an R&B singer looking for a contract, and me, the entrepreneur. I almost don't fit into this group. My t-shirt and jeans are the simplest of the lot, and while I might look decent enough for women to not ask why the hell I was on the page in the first place, I know I was selected primarily to rep for the business brothas, not the model brothas.

I close the magazine and put it under the counter. "What time is Ray-Ray coming in?"

"He called in saying he had to drive his girl to the dentist. She's getting her wisdom teeth taken out or something."

"Does he even own a car?"

"Shit, I don't know," J says, reaching under the counter for the magazine and continuing to scan the issue.

"If you ever give me the green light, you know I'm gonna kick that brotha to the curb," I say.

Ray-Ray has been the subject of a never-ending discussion between J and me. The only reason he is even here is because J feels we need to have one actual employee in order for us to consider ourselves legit entrepreneurs. Apparently, if you have no one to call you "boss," then what's the point?

Even if we needed an employee, I thought we could do a lot better than Ray-Ray's silly ass, but every time J mentioned that no one else would take a job with so little money and keep coming around, I had to just nod and agree. It was clear that Ray-Ray couldn't live off of what we were paying him. Hell, we were barely getting by ourselves.

"The new website launches this Friday. This merch shit better work or we'll have to see if we can keep the doors open," J says, not looking up from a picture of Kerry Washington.

I nod, scanning the space of our small shop. We have no customers and a room full of CDs, t-shirts, posters, and stickers. Lalah Hathaway's heavy, raspy voice sings "For Always" through the speakers in the upper corners of the shop.

"Dude," I say. "Riddle me this: why in the world would we open a record shop in 2010? We must be the dumbest Morehouse Men in history."

J looks up from the magazine. "Cool, you gotta have faith. This store might sell music, but make no mistake, brotha, this is much more than a record shop."

✿

ANY BROTHA AT THE AGE OF THIRTY WHO IS still single is single for a reason. That's not to say there was never "the one"—chances are there was—but something happened to mess everything up. And once a sista has whipped your heart like Denzel in *Glory*, it's easy to shoot the deuces to the idea of true love.

My story went something like that.

I was a senior at Morehouse and head-over-heels in love with this sista from Spelman named Rhonda. This was the way I dreamed it would go down: we'd get married at Dansforth Chapel on Morehouse's campus, the customary spot for "Spel-house" hook-ups, move to the outskirts of Charlotte, have some crumb-snatchers, and spend our days sipping sweet tea on the porch of a renovated antebellum house. Damn, I was naive. I don't know which part stung the most: the fact that she was cheating on me with a football player from Georgia Tech or the fact that he had gotten her pregnant. I had been strapping up with her since day one—thank God—but she had been letting this other dude raw-dog her the entire time. Needless to say, that was the last serious relationship I had ever been in, and that was over nine years ago.

Not that there hadn't been opportunities to have something serious with someone else along the way. I just didn't want it. I'd be a fool if someone else got a chance to run that number on me again. It's like they say, "First time, shame on you. Second time, shame on me." And I'll be damned if I have to sing that tune again.

One of the ironies about dating is that I can be honest about all of this up front. But no matter how many times I tell a woman that I don't want anything serious, she keeps soldiering on under the mistaken assumption that she can be the one woman who can change my mind. It took a lot of experiences for me to get to this point, so it's beyond me why anyone would think I just hadn't met the right person. No, I had met her. It was just that she decided to do a number on me. And whether that's holding all women guilty for something that one woman did, so be it. My pops used to say it's okay to sleep with a snake…as long as you know where the head is.

When the editor from *Soul Sista* called about being one of their twenty-five most eligible bachelors, I was going to pass, but J was convinced it would be a good look for our business. He had said, "Cool, you see what being on a list like that does for actors in Hollywood? All we need is just a little bit of that at our store." I guess in his mind he figured women would just trek up here to Harlem to look at the guy from the magazine profile and maybe buy a CD before they left.

I can't blame him though. He coordinates the marketing for C&J's Rare Grooves, so I'm just doing my part. But I hope no one really takes seriously the idea that I'm looking for that special someone, even if she does turn out to be the embodiment of a Stevie Wonder song.

The idea for C&J's Rare Grooves didn't originate in Harlem. It actually started in Atlanta.

During one of my trips down to the ATL for Morehouse's homecoming weekend, I had heard about a small record shop in Little Five Points called Moods Music. Because my taste in music tends to stray from the radio, I was impressed to find that they carried so many neo-soul artists I had discovered only by downloading the occasional "grown & sexy" mixtape. In that first trip, I must have dropped more than $500. It was only after my third visit to the store in five years that my college roommate, Julian, proposed that we launch a similar type of store in our Harlem neighborhood, since there wasn't anything exactly like it around. My vision was immediately clouded with images of Raphael Saadiq, Dwele, Eric Roberson, Conya Doss, and Ledisi doing CD signings, while lines of soul fans wrapped around the block. We jumped in head first, leaving behind our jobs at our respective investment banking firms.

I can still remember the day I submitted my

letter of resignation to my boss, Grant Fields. At first he laughed.

"What the fuck is this?" he finally managed, when he saw I wasn't laughing along with him.

"I'm leaving to start a business."

He stared at me for a moment before leaning in closely, his eyes squinting. "You know there's a non-compete clause in your employment contract."

That had always bothered me when I went to work at the firm, but I suspected that I couldn't work as an analyst forever, so I went along with it. Hearing Grant toss it back in my face irked me a little, but I shrugged it off.

"I'm opening a store with a friend."

"Really?" Grant said, lightening up. "What are you going to sell?"

"Music. Soul music."

Grant shook his head, his black moussed hair looking like a plastic helmet atop his pale face. "Good luck with that," he offered sarcastically.

I started to tell him all of the things I had stored in the back of my mind for a day like this, all of the curse words and names I had come up with for him in the last eight years. Instead, I only muttered the word "fucker" under my breath as I turned away from him, and I seriously doubt he even heard it.

At least I was now free to explore my dream.

It had taken J and me a while to get everything set up, but now we've been open for about eight months. Business has been pretty dismal. It turns out that we found a niche market, but most of our market would rather buy their albums much cheaper on iTunes, and we can't compete with that. Somewhere in the past few months we got the idea to create merchandise for the store and hired a freshman at Parsons to create a few designs. Now we're moving just as much merchandise as we are music, which, while encouraging, isn't saying much.

Just last week a woman dropped by the store looking for a Beyonce CD and wound up getting into an altercation with Ray-Ray in the process.

"Where y'alls Beyonce stuff at?" the woman huffed.

"We don't carry Beyonce in here. This is a specialty shop for real soul music, lady."

"Y'all ain't got no Beyonce? What the hell kinda record store ain't got no Beyonce?"

"We deal primarily with independent artists and smaller labels," Ray-Ray said, sticking to the script we wrote for him for just this type of occasion.

"Y'all got all these black folks ain't nobody ever heard of, and y'all ain't got no Beyonce? Well, do y'all got some Chris Brown?"

"No Chris Brown either. We have some good stuff in here though. Ever heard of The Foreign Exchange?" Ray-Ray said.

"The Foreign who? Y'all trippin' up in here. Y'all need some Beyonce or Chris Brown."

Finally, Ray-Ray lost his cool. "If you want that pop shit, then take your ass down to K-Mart. They got plenty of it over there. Good prices, too."

"Don't tell me where to take my ass, mother-fucker," the woman started, before I came around the counter and apologized for Ray-Ray's comment. I even offered her a free t-shirt, but she responded, "Y'all ain't gonna have me out here in these streets advertising for y'all's asses and y'all ain't got no Beyonce!"

The biggest ray of light for C&J's Rare Grooves in the days after *Soul Sista* hit the newsstand, though, was the mail the magazine forwarded me. Apparently, a lot of women were struck by that profile and a few went on to place orders online.

"See? That's what I was saying," J said, after he started to run the numbers. "I wish they could put your ass in every issue."

We had a good laugh back then, but in these three weeks since the issue came out, we've moved more product this month than in the last three months combined.

Some of the letters included pictures, some like glamour shots, others of women standing on beaches in bathing suits. One of J's favorite games is sorting through the various pictures telling me which ones I should make a play for. I don't plan on following through on any of them, although some of them are pretty fine.

Most of the letters read the same way. Woman X is looking for a real man, one who can appreciate the delicate flower she is. (Okay, I'm being a little "extra" here.) Some of them even quoted lyrics from their favorite Stevie Wonder songs. One woman went so far as to record herself onto a CD singing "Overjoyed." She didn't sound too bad either, but I have no idea of what she plans for me to do with that CD. We're a record store, not a record label.

J suggested that we send each of the women a flyer for the store, but I think that would be kind of crass. It seems like a poor consolation, if you ask me, especially if you had your hopes set on something more, like making a romantic connection.

❧

I LIVE IN A ONE-BEDROOM APARTMENT IN A brownstone off of St. Nicholas, just a few blocks from the A/C 145th Street subway station. It's a pretty decent neighborhood and becoming more gentrified by the day—but what part of Harlem isn't these days? There are more whites than blacks on my block, and the look of 125th Street these days reminds all who visit that Bill Clinton still has a presence here.

Still beautiful Black faces of every shade abound, reminding me of the rich history of the area. But it's much more than that. Harlem has a kind of spirit—energy—that permeates every crack in the sidewalk, ever light bulb in a sign, and every neighborhood stoop. Most of the people are good, hardworking people, and being from the South, I can appreciate that a great deal. But I'm no fool. I know that New York is not Mississippi and that there must be a reason for the bulletproof glass at the neighborhood Popeye's Chicken.

How J and I both wound up in Harlem is a whole other story altogether. We were roommates in college and both accepted job offers on Wall Street. Although we both ended up moving to Harlem, we opted to get our own places. Still it's ironic that we would go into business together. Now we see each other even more than we did in college. Yes, Julian Saddler a/k/a "J" is my brother, my right hand, my ace boon coon. I don't think I would have ventured into entrepreneurship if he hadn't been so persuasive. I'm glad that we decided to do it though. Even on days when we have only a handful of sales, it beats the long, intense hours of shuffling around non-disclosure agreements for various clients and preparing modified models for my bosses, based on the latest financial statements of whatever company I was assigned to work on. While the salary was good, if I did the math, with the number of hours I worked in any given week, I made slightly more than a manager at a fast food restaurant, and there was no job fulfillment at all.

Now, job fulfillment is about all that I do have.

***

"Chauncey, I saw your picture in the magazine. All of the women at the church are talking about it. Even that Edith Hopper—you know the girl who just finished up at Meharry Medical College. I'm telling you, you gotta settle down at some point. May as well be with a doctor," my mother says, barely taking a breath between sentences.

I squeeze my cell phone tighter and try not to roll my eyes. "We'll see," I offer as a consolation.

"You ain't getting no younger, boy. By the time you give me some grandchildren, I'll be so old I can't do nothing with 'em."

This time I do roll my eyes. Although I know she can't see my facial expression, there's a part of me that thinks my mother might still reach through the phone and pop me anyway.

Mama wants me to get married and have children—in that order—and I don't see any of that happening in the foreseeable future. Sometimes I wish that she and my father had had another child so some of the burden could have been shifted, but as fate would have it, I am the chosen one.

"And your father's not too happy that you didn't use your government name," she adds.

"People know me as Cool, not as Chauncy Carter Brown, III. I can't even fit all of that on a business card."

Mama sighs. "Don't let your daddy hear you say that. He's still holding out hope for a Chauncey Carter Brown, IV."

I laugh. My mother does not.

"So when are you going to come up here to Harlem to check out the store?" I ask.

"You guys are online now, aren't you? I can just check out everything there."

Now that my mother has a tablet computer, she's joined the demographic referred to affectionately as "the silver surfers," older people who spend a lot of their retirement time roaming the Internet.

"It's not the same as seeing it up close and in person," I offer.

"I don't know. I'm a Southern lady. I don't know if I could get around in a city that big," she says.

"It's easier than you think. Plus, I'll be here to take you around."

"Well, I'll have to check our schedule and see if we can fit it in."

Both of my parents are retired, never having left Mississippi, and their schedules are about as loose as a belt after a good meal, but they are forever allowing themselves to be scared by the news about New York on CNN. When September 11th happened, that gave Mama an eternal license to scratch the city off of her list of places to go and visit. I know they'll never come to see me now, but I can't bring myself to stop inviting them—just in case they do decide to change their minds.

"Well, just know it's a standing invitation," I say.

"Okay. Well, I have to run, but do you want me to give your number to Edith?"

"Mama, I can tell you right now that I can't do a long distance relationship."

"Chauncey, from the looks of it, you can't do a short distance one either."

Touché.

3

By the time I make it to the store, I see Ray-Ray is already moving around aimlessly, tidying things up and trying to look busy.

"Cool, you got a message on the counter. Some woman from *Soul Sista* called and left a number," he said, refolding a shirt he had already folded.

"A'ight," I respond. "Is J in the back?"

"He had to run an errand. He should be back in a few."

I walk into the back room and put a mug of water in the microwave. I pull out a green tea bag and grab a seat at the table pushed against the wall. Boxes of merchandise fill the room, and I feel a hollow pit in my stomach. I'm not sure we could sell all of this stuff—even on a good day. In fact, some days it feels like J, Ray-Ray, and I are the only ones wearing these things. It's our store uniform, so I have a stack of them in different colors in my closet at home.

When the microwaves goes off, I drop in my tea bag and head back to the main store room and cop a squat on one of the stools behind the counter. Ray-

Ray's chicken scratch is barely legible, but I can make out the phone number and the name with a little effort. I pick up the phone by the register and dial the number.

"May I speak to Denise Mallory?" I say, dipping the tea bag in the hot water a few times.

"May I ask who's calling?" a low, raspy voice answers. I can't tell if it's a man or a woman.

"This is Cool Brown. I got a message from her this morning."

"Hold please. I'll see if she's available."

A few seconds later another voice comes on the line, this one softer and more feminine.

"Hey, Mr. Brown. This is Denise Mallory."

"You can just call me Cool. Mr. Brown's my father," I say to lighten the mood.

"All right, *Cool*," she responds, my name fitting in her mouth awkwardly. "Can I ask you why they call you that?"

"I picked it up when I pledged back in college. My big brothers said I didn't get fazed easily. Like Big Boi said, 'Cooler than a polar bear's toenails,' you know?"

"Well, all righty then," she responds, and I can't tell if she's amused or if she could care less.

She continues, "The reason I'm calling you is because we have been getting a lot of letters and e-mails for you in behind that bachelor spread we ran in the last issue. We've been forwarding them to your work address. Have you been getting them?"

I chuckle. "Yeah. I got them."

"So I guess you already know how popular you are with our readers."

"I figured the other guys were getting the same type of mail, like it came with the territory."

"Well, I can assure you that's not the case," Denise answers. "The funny part is that there are even more e-mails that we've gotten that simply ask about you. No personal notes or anything. Just people who are curious."

I take a sip of my tea. "I guess I should be flattered then."

"I would, if I were you. We keep getting women who say that your profile was witty, that you are nice looking, and that you have a really relaxed persona. That seems to be a winning combination for many women."

"They could get all of that from a blurb and a picture?" I ask.

"Women are perceptive like that."

I can see Ray-Ray watching me out the corner of his eye while he cuts open a box of CDs.

"So you were calling for my e-mail address then?"

"Not exactly," she says. "I have a proposition for you."

I AM INCREDULOUS AS I LOWER THE PHONE. By now, Ray-Ray is looking directly at me. I lift the receiver to my mouth again and ask, "Are you serious?"

"Very much so," she responds.

Now I wish J would hurry up and get back here, because if he thought being profiled in the magazine in the first place was major, he will turn back flips up and down 125th Street when he hears this.

"How would this work?" I ask.

"We would give you a column on the website's homepage that you would update weekly. All you'd have to do is go on three dates with women selected by our readers."

I can sense the complications already, but the exposure would do wonders for C&J's Rare Grooves. It's not like she's pulling a *Fear Factor* and asking me to eat a one hundred-year-old ostrich egg. This is just three little dates.

"Does the magazine foot the bill?" I ask.

"Up to one hundred for each of the first three dates," she responds.

"But this is New York. I'm gonna need more."

"Be creative. You can make it work."

I sigh as I consider this. "Well, would I write all of the details down on the blog, kind of like the tell-all thing they do on *The Dating Game*?"

"I would say yes. The editor-in-chief wants you to do something like a reality show, except as an on-line column."

"Like *Flavor of Love*," I say.

She laughs. "You don't look anything like Flavor Flav, but I guess you could say that."

"Are these women from the area or will they be flown in, and if so, how am I supposed to deal with that?"

"The readers will ultimately decide, but I suspect that most, if not all, of the women will be from the New York City area, simply because our demographics in this area are pretty strong, especially with the website."

I already know that I'm going to say yes, but I tell her that I'll think on it and call her back after lunch today.

When J finally strolls into the store a half hour later, I tell him, "Guess what, dude?"

He looks at me curiously.

"I get to be Boris Kodjoe for longer than a month."

AFTER I REPLAY THE CONVERSATION IN ITS entirety, J sits down, a huge smile on his face. "You do know what this means, right?" he says.

I have a feeling I know, but I ask him anyway.

"We get repeat advertising through their site. Hell, every time they run your column, the words 'C&J's Rare Grooves' will appear beneath your name. Do you realize the number of baby t-shirts we could sell if you play your cards right? Cool, just imagine," he says, placing a hand on my shoulder, "if that box in the back actually went empty and we had to reorder!"

My heart starts to race. We can do this, I tell myself. We can turn this sinking ship around.

"You've got to be the quintessential gentleman, though. Women aren't gonna want to buy shirts from a dude who has the rep of some playboy," he says, unable to catch his breath. "Oh yeah, and you've gotta wear one of our shirts in the profile picture. Maybe throw a blazer over it. We've gotta get you a haircut, too."

"What's wrong with my hair?" I ask.

"Nothing—if you don't mind that the back of

your neck looks like ground beef. We need you looking like Steve Harvey's old barber hooked you up. From here forward I command you to wear a doo-rag. Gotta get those waves goin'."

"Well, dude, tell me how you *really* feel!" I say, shaking my head.

Ray-Ray walks over and leans against the counter. "You know people are gonna expect you to find a soulmate out of this or something."

Leave it to Ray-Ray to piss on our parade, but I know he's right.

We won't get any of this publicity for free. It will only cost me one thing: my personal life.

4

———

I met Rhonda, the woman who drove a stake through my heart like I was a vampire, during the summer before my senior year at Morehouse. She was a rising junior at Spelman, where she majored in English. She was spending her summer working at an indie bookstore downtown called Maggie's Nook, and although we'd probably crossed paths a few hundred times going back and forth between our two campuses, it took me randomly walking into the bookstore on a June afternoon for us to officially meet.

She was working the customer service kiosk, which, in a store that small, looked like it could have been a coat-check closet at a restaurant. The atmosphere was warm and cozy, the way I imagined some small English bookseller's shop to be. Still Rhonda looked too fine to be tucked away back there. Part of my reason for speaking to her in the first place was because I was checking to see if they carried a photography coffee table book by Marc Baptiste. It turned out that they didn't, but she was aware of the photographer, and our little banter about his work led to her telling me about her own interest in photography. She was an art major, but she had just gotten her hands on a DSLR camera and was hoping to do a lot of shooting that summer.

If it had not been for the connection we made while talking about photography, I probably wouldn't have had the nerve to ask for her phone number, but I'm glad that I did. That turned out to be one of the best summers of my life.

It started casually with late night conversations on the phone, us whispering to each other until the early hours of the morning, cell phone batteries running low, and our having to camp out next to outlets so we could keep the conversation going while we recharged. She talked about growing up in Oakton, Virginia, secretly crushing on Shel Silverstein when she was younger, and being addicted to Roald Dahl's children stories. I told her about growing up in Mississippi, just across the Tennessee state line in Corinth, and about how I had always wanted to own my own business. Eventually I pushed the envelope one evening after we'd been on the phone for over three hours.

"You know, we could be having this conversation face-to-face," I said, lying on my bed in only my boxers.

"I guess you're right," she responded, playing along.

"Would you like to come over?"

"Are you serious? It's almost midnight."

"What time do you go in to work tomorrow?"

"I'm off tomorrow," she said.

"So you have nothing to lose then."

As she pondered my offer, I added, "I don't bite.

We could even leave here and grab something to eat at Waffle House or IHOP."

"I'm not even dressed right now. It would take me at least thirty minutes to get myself together," she said.

"I'm not going anywhere. I can even stay on the phone with you while you drive or if you want, I can pick you up."

She finally asked where I lived.

"Just off of Cascade, not too far from the school."

"I'll come over there. I just don't like to be without my car. It's not you or anything. Just the way I do things."

"I understand."

Within the hour, her car pulled up to my first floor apartment, and I met her in the doorway. It was the first time that I had ever touched her. After hours of talking to her, I felt like I knew her, so when I lowered my head to kiss her lips, it felt as natural as breathing. She responded to my kiss warmly, her arms wrapped around my bare shoulders.

Right then I knew there was no turning back. She had me.

OVER THE COURSE OF THAT SUMMER THERE were many firsts: our first kiss, our first date, our first road trip, our first time making love. It seemed as if everything around us was poetry in the making. There wasn't a love song in the world that I wouldn't have dedicated to her. Some nights we would just hop in my car, pop Jill Scott in the CD player, and drive up Interstate 85, just so we could turn around and drive back towards the city, catching the brilliant lights of the downtown skyline.

Shortly before school started back, we were lying in my bed after making love, the candles still flickering softly around us, and I told her that I loved her. She looked at me for what seemed like the longest moment in my life before finally responding, "I love you, too."

I wanted to ask her what took her so long to respond, but I was just so happy to hear the words at all. The fact that she took the time to consider her feelings before responding was a good thing, I reasoned. That way it was more genuine.

❧

REPLAYING EVERYTHING THAT HAPPENED LATER on, I question whether I could've figured things out much earlier. In my mind, our relationship was perfect. I had opened a romantic vein and bled poetry, flowers, and compliments on a daily basis. I did everything that I had ever dreamed of doing for the woman I would marry. And on her end, there weren't any signs that I could've picked up on. Our sex life was regular, exciting, and, as far as I knew, monogamous. If she hadn't gotten pregnant, I don't think she would've ever told me the truth about the other guy.

When she revealed to me that she was pregnant, I immediately assumed it was mine. Why wouldn't I? And even though I knew having a child would alter our futures, I loved her enough to accept that. I went to embrace her when she stepped back away from me.

"It's not yours," she said.

"What?"

I collapsed onto my couch, my head buried in my hands, unable to look at her while she paced back and forth in front of me telling me about this other guy, about how she was confused, about how he was her ex-boyfriend and how they were on "break" when I had met her.

"You were doing it raw with him the whole time?" I asked. I don't know why I fixed myself to even ask that question, especially with the answer being so obvious, but I guess at that moment in time I just had to hear it from her own lips.

"He was my first."

It wasn't really an answer, but I guess in a strange way, it was.

It took me much longer than I'd ever care to admit to officially put Rhonda in my rearview mirror, but even with her floating aimlessly in my past, I learned a valuable lesson: even on my absolute best behavior, a woman would still cheat on me. I figured if both men and women could cheat on their significant others, then what was the point in making a serious commitment? You can only really get hurt if you put yourself out there.

I picked Rhonda, and she ripped my heart in two like a voided check. Now the readers of *Soul Sista* magazine will pick three women for me, in hopes of my finding a soulmate in one of their choices. It's almost comical when you think about it.

I'll take it a date at a time, but I'm not expecting my world to do a 180-degree flip any time soon.

5

———

"I can't believe you're gonna let them pimp you like that," Angie says between bites of her panini.

"It's not really pimping. I'm just writing a column. Plus, I get to keep my business in front of potential customers without coming out of pocket," I respond.

"Call it what you want, but you're being sent out there like a prostitute on the strip to go on dates with women that you don't know." She laughs. "And you're getting *paid* to do it."

"Come on! They're giving me a per diem, not a paycheck."

"Next thing you know, the people over at *Soul Sista* will be telling you to walk between the raindrops to get them their stories." She holds her head back so that she doesn't spray food in my face from her laughter.

I shake my head. I don't know what I expected Angie to tell me. She has always been my sounding board, and being that she's my cousin, I can talk to her without complication. I look at her, and she lowers her head, eyeing me as if to say, "You know I'm right."

"But what if, hypothetically speaking, I meet a woman who winds up being *the one*? Would you still think I'm being pimped?"

"You have about as much of a chance of finding the one as I have of going back to dick," she says, cackling again.

"That's fucked up, you know," I say, trying to conceal my smile.

I pick at my salad, mixing the romaine and spinach into patterns of dark and light greens.

"Don't look so sad, Cool. I'm just messing with you. Who knows? This might be what you need to shake things up in your life," she offers in the way of sarcastic consolation.

To change the subject, I offer, "The website re-launched. We have more t-shirts and other merchandise. And of course music."

"I'm gonna have to head Uptown to check you guys out. It's just been so busy with Tracy and the baby. I'm still trying to match my sleep patterns with Aaron's, 'cause if I don't, I won't get any sleep at all."

"How is my little cousin doing?" I ask.

"If I can get him to stop pissing in my face every time I change his diapers, I'd be doing something major."

"Well, maybe you should've been the one to have the baby then," I say.

"Hell, no," she responds, slapping the table and laughing. "Tracy handles pain a lot better than me. I don't mind a little piss in the face anyway. I hear that shit clears up the skin."

I raise my hands up and down imitating a scale.

"Piss in the face versus being pimped," I say. "We must be the pride and joy of our family."

"Hey, it is what it is, right?" she says, pushing her braids away from her round face.

I nod.

Her smile disappears, and for the first time since we sat down to eat, she looks serious. "Cool, I know I don't say this too often, but I'm glad you came to New York." She puts what's left of her sandwich back onto her plate. "I just feel so out of touch with everyone in the family, you know. It's good seeing a face that looks like mine."

I reach for her hand and hold it. "I got you, cuz."

I don't ask her when was the last time that she went home to Alabama. I don't even ask her when was the last time she talked to Aunt Jonetta. Some things are just best left alone.

As we leave the restaurant, I give her a big hug, then turn to walk back to the subway station. Her voice calls out loudly from behind me.

"Cool?"

"Yeah," I respond, turning my head.

"Everything will work out."

I don't know what she's referring to specifically, but the advice seems to hit nearly everything in my life all at once.

I nod.

"Love you, cuz," I say, waving goodbye.

She smiles. "Love you, too, Chauncey."

My face twists up at hearing my name, but my cousin is already laughing as she walks back across the street to work.

When I make it back Uptown to the store, the first thing I do is break out my laptop and check *Soul Sista*'s website. I am curious to see if they have already started the voting process. Sure enough, on the homepage of the website on the right sidebar is a small photograph of me with the words "*Soul Sista*'s Own Bachelor." I know it is a reference to the television show, but the words by themselves remind me of Angie's words: *they are pimping you.* There I am smiling like a happy little ho. Beneath my picture is the name "Cool Brown" and no mention of "C&J's Rare Grooves, Harlem" anywhere. My heart sinks, and I find myself reaching blindly for the phone.

"Cool Brown calling for Denise Mallory, please," I say, before I am put on hold.

When she answers, I try to maintain my professionalism, but I'm simmering beneath the surface. After our customary greetings, I immediately cut to the chase. "I thought we agreed that my business would be listed under my name."

"It's not on there?" she asks. "I sent the information over to our webmaster."

I breathe a sigh of relief. At least it doesn't appear to be deliberate. "I just checked the site, and it's not there."

"I tell you what. Let me check on that right quick, and I'll give you a call back in a minute."

As I hang up the phone, I try to relax to the sounds of Anthony David playing in the background. I can hear J in the back room typing away on his laptop, working on our marketing plan. Ray-Ray has already left for the day, and only a handful of people are standing around, combing through our music racks.

"If you need any help or recommendations, just holler," I offer.

The brother with the dredlocks turns my way and nods. "Respect," he says, turning back to the CDs. "Hey, mon, this Electric Conversation nice?"

"Definitely," I respond. "Lyrics in English and French. Dilla influence. Definitely good stuff."

He and his lady friend approach the register with the CD.

"Mon, dis no good, me comes back," he says, laughing.

"You'll like it. Trust me," I say smiling.

"Hey, you're that guy from *Soul Sista*," his lady friend says, her accent sounding like she could have grown up somewhere down South, near me.

I nod while ringing up the CD.

"See, I told you that was him," she says, nudging the guy.

I put the CD in a bag along with the receipt.

"Mon, dey come for you now," the guy says.

"Who?"

"De sharks," he says, laughing. "De women, dey smell blood in da water."

"Dexter, leave that man alone," the woman says. Then she turns to me. "But if you're looking, I have a girlfriend who's about five-seven. She's cute, too. Great smile."

Dexter gently tugs her arm and leads her toward the door. "He have his hands full," he says, tickled.

When they leave, I hear J rise from his laptop and stretch his tall, lanky frame. He runs his fingers through his low haircut and walks into the main room, copping a squat next to me. "Did I hear you say that *Soul Sista* is tripping about putting our name on the website?"

"It was just a mistake. Denise is checking on everything right now and is supposed to call me back in a few minutes."

"Okay. Don't get my heart rate up, Cool. I thought I was going have to hop in a cab and go down there to see what's up," J says, his eyes still a little glazed over from typing on his laptop for the past hour.

"So how is the new and improved marketing plan coming?" I ask.

"I'm thinking we should have an open-mic poetry event here once a month."

I look around the room and imagine people standing all over the store. I try to visualize where our stage area would be. No matter how I turn the idea around in my head, the room just feels too small to cram a bunch of people in here. People would have to stand, if this thing actually caught on.

"Can we even fit enough people in here to make it worth our while?" I ask.

"That's the beauty of it. We market it so that people know that everything will be going down in a small, intimate space."

"What are you gonna call it? Poetry in the Closet?"

J shakes his head, his expression serious. "I actually thought about that, but I didn't want to offend any gay people."

"What?"

"In the closet."

It takes me a moment to realize what he's talking

about. "Jesus, dude! Well, what about Poetry Out of the Closet?" I say, laughing. "Okay, you just tell me what else you came up with."

"The Poetry Vault," J says, but he doesn't seem confident.

"Sounds kind of confining. Like we're all trapped in a bank vault or something. People might start to feel claustrophobic in here," I say.

"Well, shit. Do you at least think the idea for the open mic would work?"

"I'm definitely willing to give it a shot," I respond. "Hey, what about 'C&J's Rare Poetry'?"

J pauses as he considers this. "It beats the names I came up with, but I still want to do some more brainstorming."

Just as J finishes his statement, the phone rings.

"I hope this is Denise," I say, picking up the phone. "C&J's Rare Grooves," I answer.

"May I speak to Cool Brown?"

"This is he."

"Cool, this is Denise. I just finished meeting with our editor-in-chief, and I think we have a slight problem."

I swallow hard.

"They left the name of your business off the website on purpose."

6

———

Not two seconds after I hang up the phone, J asks, "So are you gonna handle this, or do I need to?"

The question makes little sense, since ultimately all of this is on me. I tell him that Denise agreed to meet with me at her office downtown to discuss my concerns in person.

I hop the A train and take it to Midtown. As I glance at the scrap of paper that I wrote the address on, I try to steel myself.

Inhale. Exhale.

I wander through the mazes of skyscrapers, trying not to come to a complete stop while taking in the beautiful, majestic structures. It's one thing to see the skyline while driving from Jersey into the Lincoln Tunnel, but walking *in* the actual skyline itself is incredible. Each street has its own character, so the walk is never boring. And after being here as long as I have, I am constantly surprised at the fact that I can always find something that I haven't seen before. It's as if the city simply evolves around you.

As I turn off of Broadway and its bustling scene

of tourists and locals, I spot Denise's building with no problem. When I walk in, I let the meaty red-headed guy behind the desk know that I am there to see Denise Mallory. He hands me a visitor sticker and has me sign in.

"Take the elevator to the fifth floor," he says, before returning to his magazine.

As I walk around the corner to the elevator, I muse at the irony of *Soul Sista* being on the fifth floor of the building. Where I am from, the "fifth floor" is our down-home way of saying the mental ward. I wonder for a moment if these people will be crazy, and I have to remind myself that I am there to clear up something that should have been resolved from our initial conversation. So maybe I am walking into a mental ward after all.

I step off the elevator on the fifth floor, and the foyer is swanked out with graphite colored walls and a large brushed steel *Soul Sista* logo illuminated from behind with red light. Two long leather couches are positioned, facing each other with a coffee table between them. The table is covered with several copies of the last few issues. A tall, thin receptionist is positioned in the corner, and there is a large door off to her side, the entrance to the actual office space, I presume.

"My name is Cool Brown, and I'm here to see Denise Mallory," I say.

She nods. "You are one of the bachelors, right?" Her raspy voice sounds like she sings bass for a barbershop quartet. I immediately recognize it from when I called earlier.

"Yes, I'm one of the bachelors," I say, unsure I will still be one when I leave this office.

"Have a seat over there," she says, pointing at the couches, "and she will be with you in a moment."

I sit down and settle into the cushions, the seat rising up around my legs. The leather is still warm, as if some big guy had been sitting there just before I arrived.

The door opens and a brown skin woman with an Afro puff pulled back walks into the reception area. She's wearing a pair of thin, cat-eyed glasses and has the look of a soul singer merged with an old librarian. The 'frohemian librarian, I muse, as she introduces herself.

"I'm Denise," she says, shaking my hand. "I hope you didn't have any trouble finding this place."

"Not at all."

She is very friendly as she ushers me through the door and around a maze of cubicles. We step into her office, a small white box with a window that only has a view of the same floor of the building across the street.

"Not to be too direct," I start, "but I don't understand what happened in the time between when you asked me to do this and now."

She closes the door and takes a seat at her desk. I sit down across from her.

"The editor-in-chief is taking the position that you're trying to occupy a prime advertising space. She even wanted us to airbrush the logo off of the t-shirt you were wearing in the picture," she says, her voice low and hushed.

"I can't believe this is even an issue," I say, not attempting to match her volume. "You have our permission to use our logo in the picture, and you're not even paying me for writing the column. As for the byline, it's like this, if we can't agree to keep all of the information in, then you'll just have to use another one of your bachelors."

"But we've already finished the voting process for you," she says, her eyes clearly pained at having to get the horse back into the barn.

"All you guys have to do is hold up your end of the deal and everything goes back to normal. I mean we're only talking about two words, two letters, and an ampersand. How much are you guys really losing in advertising. You can even leave the 'Harlem' part off, although I'm guessing that part actually works to your advantage."

Denise lowers her head, staring at a pencil that she's twirling between her thin fingers. She's quiet for a moment before she lifts her eyes to meet mine. "Cool, I'm on your side," she finally admits, her voice still hushed and controlled. "You're right. We had a deal. The editor-in-chief is reneging, if I can be honest."

"Yeah," I whisper conspiratorially. "I hate re-negers." It sounds comical and almost racist when I hear the word fall from my lips.

When she smiles, I realize two things: (1) I have an ally, and (2) her smile is absolutely gorgeous.

She leans forward, "I'll tell you what. I'm going to go back and convince Rachel that we need to move forward with our original agreement—since the website is already set up—and I'll make sure that you get your byline the way you want it. You know what this means, though?"

"I guess it means I have to have some pretty interesting dates, or at least write them that way."

There goes that smile again, and for a moment I

nearly forget about all of the grief that brought me to this office in the first place.

"Are you curious to see who the readers have selected for you to go out with?"

"I guess," I say, my stomach already anxious. "Can I see the picture and the bio for my first date?"

"Sure." She opens one of the three filing folders on her desk. "The first one is a sister named Sarah." She slides the folder across to me.

The first thing that strikes me about the photograph is how bold the woman is standing in the photograph, her back erect, hands on her hips, legs spaced slightly wider than her shoulders. She looks like a model. Her dark complexion and low twists create a striking image when viewed within the profile of her compact and athletic frame. She's clearly a woman far too stylish and beautiful to be plucked from a random group of women who simply wrote in. I turn my head a little. "Do I know her from somewhere?"

"She's a principal with the Dance Theater of Harlem."

"And she wants to go out with me? This sista looks like she could have any man she wants."

Denise nods. "They all do."

"I guess I should thank all of those people who voted then."

I consider asking to see the information on the other women, but I decide against it. I'll play it straight using the rules that the magazine came up with. I won't even bother to Facebook these women. I figure what I learn about them will either come from the *Soul Sista* files or from the dates themselves. It would be a lot more interesting that way.

Denise chuckles softly. "Maybe you'll find that special someone." Her voice is not all that convincing.

"Do you really believe I'll find someone out of this collection of random women?" I ask, sarcasm dripping from my voice. I figure I can be honest now that it feels like we are on the same team.

"Hey, what do I know?" she responds, her eyes dancing behind her glasses. "This is New York City. Anything can happen."

7

DATE ONE

SARAH

I called ahead to Charli's, a swanky restaurant on the Upper West Side, and made a reservation. I wanted to start out strong, although I knew I had run the risk of using up my entire one hundred dollar per diem. Denise had come through in flying colors, getting the website updated with my business info, so I was in great spirits. I even figured if the date went well enough, I could come out of my pocket a little, if need be. I'm sure J would figure out a tax deduction from the receipts.

After the cab pulls up to the curb in front of the restaurant, I get my first complete front, back, and side views of Sarah. She is about five-foot-six in her heels. The simple, yet elegant, black dress she is wearing falls on her frame in such a way that it's impossible not to know that she's a professional dancer. The twists in her hair form an ornate crown, and with her posture, I feel as though I'm escorting a queen.

Prior to getting my notes on Sarah, I had posed a question to Denise.

"Am I just supposed to go on three dates and

pick someone to start a relationship with? If so, that sounds like Hoopz standing there with that silly ass grill in her mouth waiting for her five minute relationship with Flav to end."

Denise responded, "If a date goes well, see where it goes. Just make sure you go on each one at least once."

There were at least two major things wrong with what she said. First, I couldn't figure how I was supposed to get to know any of these women with the others waiting in the wings. Second, the whole thing felt like I was herding them through a process that wasn't fair to anyone. Meanwhile, I was supposed to write a blog entry every week about how things were going with each of them. One thing was for damned sure: the idea sounded much better on paper than it did when you had to go and execute it.

Now I'm sitting across from Sarah Landfair who is dressed to impress and clearly ready for a real date, not some Hollywood set-up. She wasn't sent here from central casting, and she doesn't seem to be here for any other reason than to see if we have anything in common. I immediately feel like a fraud and ask to be excused from the table.

"Is everything okay?" she asks.

"I just have to use the restroom. I'll be right back." My delivery is stilted and awkward, but she nods as if she understands.

I work my way across the restaurant to the restroom/lounge area, taking out my phone along the way. I quickly punch in J's number and push the "CALL" button.

"Hello?"

"J, I can't do this!"

"What? Who? Man, pull yourself together!" J says, finally realizing it's me.

"Sorry, but I can't go through with this. Dude, this sista is here for a real date. This is no game."

"Well, have a real date then, Cool. Ain't that the point?" he responds, nonplused.

Up until that moment, all of this had been largely an elaborate production in my mind, even though I knew what was at stake.

"Yeah," I mumble into the receiver.

J sighs. "Just enjoy your date. Have fun and worry about the technicalities tomorrow."

"You're right," I say, thanking him and hanging up the phone.

I return to the table and take a seat across from Sarah, unsure of what to do next. I feel as though we have been dropped in the middle of a prop. The only thing that's missing is the camera crew. I can hear what J would say in the back of my head, "There *are* no cameras, so don't sweat it."

Sarah looks at me, and I can tell that she's starting to get uneasy about all of this.

"You look amazing," I offer.

She smiles and thanks me, before looking away. I'm losing her interest now, I can tell.

"Well, I have an idea," I say. "Why don't we ask each other a few questions to break the ice? You can start first, and we can go back and forth."

She looks at me, pauses, then nods. "Okay. So why are you single?"

She doesn't ask it in a way that makes me feel like I'm too good to be single. It's more like she's questioning my motives for taking her out.

Feeling no need to hide anything, I say, "I was

once in love with a woman who broke my heart. She was my college sweetheart, and she cheated on me."

"How far back was this?" she asks.

"Nope. It's my turn," I say smiling. "I get to ask you a question now."

Sarah nods. "Fair enough."

"How long have you been dancing?"

She lifts her head, considering this. "It feels like I've been dancing ever since I could stand up, but I've been taking formal lessons since I was five."

"Nice," I say. "Your turn."

"How far back was your relationship with your ex-girlfriend?" she asks, without hesitation.

"Nine years."

"Nine years?" she repeats.

"Okay. My turn. What made you want to go out on this date?"

She smiles. "You just looked like someone with a good heart. All of the other guys looked like they were trying too hard, with their expensive suits and labels, and there you were, standing there in a t-shirt and jeans. You looked like someone who had no pretense, like you really just wanted to meet someone cool and down to earth. I guess I was looking for the same thing."

I nod. This is my first time hearing anyone's impression of my profile, so I take it in quietly, considering what to ask next.

"How long ago were you involved in a serious relationship?"

"About a year," she responds.

"What happened?" I ask.

"Unh unh. It's my turn."

I smile.

Before she opens her mouth, our server appears to take our orders. I'm surprised when she orders a grilled chicken Caesar salad, and I decide to do the same because I'd hate to be eating a filet mignon and lobster tail while she's picking at a salad.

After the server walks away, I say, "A salad? You could've ordered something with more sustenance."

"I'm a dancer. I have to watch what I eat. But you should've ordered what you really wanted."

"I'm good. I figure if you can eat a salad and look that amazing, then maybe I could see what a salad would do for me."

"You look just fine to me," she says.

I smile.

"So where were we?" she asks.

"I think it was your turn," I say, unable to remember exactly what we had just been talking about.

She smiles. "I've been burning to ask you this one question: what exactly does it mean when you say you want your dream woman to be the embodiment of a Stevie Wonder lyric?"

I should've expected this question at some point in time, but I'm totally unprepared to answer it. "Well," I stumble, "To be honest, I don't really know what that means. There's a part of me that feels there's a Stevie Wonder song for every occasion, like it's just the soundtrack running in the background of my life. I guess having a woman who embodies a Stevie Wonder lyric would be like having a woman who is the perfect complement to my life."

She turns her head slightly to the side so that she looks even more like a model. "Do you believe that you can find your dream woman like this? On a blind date?"

I know it's my turn for questions, but I answer anyway. "I don't know. But if I did, wouldn't that be something?"

We decide to take a walk in the warm evening air. We walk a few blocks south and stop at a coffee shop where we order two cups and sit outside at one of the small tables.

Sarah crosses her legs and leans forward. "I got one for you," she says. "It's gon' rain on yo head!"

"*The Color Purple*," I say, laughing. "Good one. What about this one? My neck! My back! My neck *and* my back!"

She laughs heartily, placing her cup on the table. "That's *Friday*! I love that movie!"

She rests her hands on her lap, and my eyes are instinctively drawn to her legs. I don't think I've ever seen a woman with legs this shapely before. Even in her dress, I can see she has a body that looks like it's been carved out of marble and buffed to a brilliant onyx shine.

"Are you from New York originally?" I ask.

"Actually, I'm from Atlanta."

"*Atlanta* Atlanta or suburban Atlanta?"

"Smyrna."

"Oh, that's not Atlanta," I say, joking. "That's Smyrna."

She shrugs her shoulders, laughing. "But most people have never heard of Smyrna."

"I used to live in Atlanta, and I can tell you right now, there's a difference."

"Oh really?" she responds, encouraging me with her smile.

"I lived off a strip of road between Campbellton and Cascade called Centra Villa, right off of the SWATS. Now that's Atlanta!"

"So do you consider Buckhead Atlanta, too? Because I'm pretty close to that area."

I smile, shaking my head. "I'll just say this: you can hang out at Lenox Mall, but for true authenticity you have to hit up Blackbriar Mall."

"I thought it was called 'Greenbriar.'"

"That's what the sign says, but have you seen all of the sneakers, weaves, and baby clothes in there?"

Sarah bends over laughing, her hand tapping the table repeatedly with each movement of her body. Her laughter is melodic and playful, and I realize that I could spend hours and hours trying to do or say things that would keep her in stitches.

"So you're from Atlanta, too?" she asks.

"Oh, no! I'm from Mississippi."

"Mississippi?" she says, more as an exclamation than a question.

"Oh, I see what this is," I say in jest. "You think I escaped slavery to get here. Well, I'll have you know that I have my papers on me right now."

She laughs heartily again, and I smile.

"What was it like growing up in Mississippi?"

"I guess just like growing up anywhere else. I don't really know how to describe it because it was all I knew. My hometown is small. It's a place called Corinth, just off of Highway 45, about forty-five miles from Tupelo. It has some pretty rich history, too. After the Civil War, a contraband camp was set up there to educate newly freed slaves."

"Impressive," she said.

"I don't know about all that."

"I mean it's impressive that you know so much about your hometown."

"Well, maybe I could show it to you one day," I venture.

She smiles. "That would be nice."

For a moment we sit quietly sipping on our coffees. I can't believe how amazing this woman is. If this were the only date I had on my schedule, I would be completely satisfied.

"So tell me about dancing. What's it like to be a professional?" I ask.

"It's hard work, but I feel fortunate that I can make a living doing it. I can't think of anything else that I've ever really felt this passionate about. It's like when I hear the music, it moves me and shapes me and spins me around. It's complete freedom."

I nod. "So what do you think about when you dance?"

She lifts her head, as if acknowledging the music of the city breathing around us. "I think Michael Jackson said it best when he talked about thinking being the worst thing a dancer can do. You have to feel it. Your body has to become one with the music. I mean, you can train and study and spend hours in the studio, but at the end of the day, dancing comes from your soul. To me, it's the best way that I can express myself."

"Well, I would love to see you dance," I say.

"I can take care of that for you. No problem."

I smile. I can only imagine what it would be like

to see her becoming one with the music, her perfect body moving in unison with the music.

"I'm really enjoying this," I say.

"So am I. Too bad you have to go on those other dates."

I take a sip from my cup, considering this. "That *is* a little crazy, isn't it?"

"Well, we both knew what we were signing up for. To tell you the truth, I didn't expect you to be this cool," she laughs. "No pun intended, Cool."

I smile. "Kind of makes me wish we could've had this date without all of the rah-rah. I'm almost afraid to step out too far now, considering I'm supposed to write about this for the website."

"How far would you have stepped out—if you weren't writing all of this down?"

It's a coy comment, I know, but seeing her sitting in that chair and knowing that we're both adults, I can't help imagining what it would feel like to lift her up and pin her against a wall. I can feel myself start to stiffen, so I quickly look back to my coffee, focusing on the heat coming through the cardboard cup.

"Damn," she says. "It's like that?"

"Who knows?" I say, laughing. "You're very attractive. You're intelligent. You're fun. I wouldn't want to keep the evening in a box."

"I feel you. So how does this work? Do I get to go out with you again, or is tonight the only time I have to make an impression on you?"

I consider what kind of impression she could make that she hasn't already made, and I feel myself stiffen again. I push away my thoughts. "From what they told me, I have to go on the three first dates, but I can see whoever I want to see again."

"But you have to write about it?"

"At least until I make my decision. I've been told that I need to make a decision at least two weeks after my third date, though."

She takes a sip from her cup. "So there's not much time to get to know anyone then."

"I guess it's just enough time to see if there's a spark of chemistry or something."

"So what do you think of me so far?"

"You're great," I respond.

"But I'm not a Stevie Wonder lyric," she says, taking another sip from her cup, her eyes flirting with me.

"We're still getting to know each other, and you could very well be."

She leans forward, her voice nearly a whisper as the taxis roll past us in the street a few feet away. "I don't believe in making out on a first date, but if I did, brotha, you would be *so* in there."

As I hear this, I realize just how much I want this woman, and it is only when I have seen her to her taxi and caught my own back to Harlem that I realize that she had planned it that way.

I lie awake on my bed listening to Jesse Boykins III's album *The Beauty Created*, my mind unable to stop thinking about Sarah. I haven't been on a real date in so long that I've almost forgotten what it feels like to be around a woman on any meaningful level. Yeah, there are women I've just "kicked it" with, but this is different. My date with Sarah felt like we had skipped the customary bullshit and cut right to the chase. We were feeling out each other for compatibility, and that was refreshing.

I wonder if it'll be the same with the other two. Will I be lying here on my bed staring at the ceiling, contemplating my feelings while listening to a quiet storm mix? If so, I might just be in over my head.

DJ Norman Jay popularized the term "rare grooves" back in the day as a part of a music show he created in England. The term had been floating around for a while before that, though. Rare grooves were those old soul tracks and B-sides that had essentially disappeared from the public consciousness. DJ Norman Jay just did like Donnie Simpson did with *Video Soul*: make a show out the scraps he had. To this day, rare groove mixes circulate the globe, finding new listeners every day.

I came up with the name C&J's Rare Grooves when I realized how many great indie artists weren't getting the exposure they deserved. Even with You-Tube and iTunes, many of them remain relatively unknown to the masses. So while African-American radio station owners battle it out with Congress about whether or not to pay a performance royalty, we have largely turned the radio off to discover our artists. The limited exposure of the artists we cover is what led us to jack the name "rare grooves."

I believe that all of this quality music deserves to be heard, and if there's any truth in Chris Anderson's Long Tail Theory (that the future of sales rests in the strong performances of smaller niches, as opposed to monster mega-hits), we should come out of this okay, albeit a little roughed-up in the process. Still when I tell people that I'm the owner of a record store, they look at me like I'm the last person on earth to get the memo, like even a seven year old knows that record stores can't survive in the digital age. The philosophy that J and I have built our business around is that there's still a strong group of people who are seeking to have a certain type of experience when they purchase, or even discover, new music. There are still people who like the idea of getting their CDs signed and buying t-shirts of their favorite artists or t-shirts of their favorite record store. We are purely niche, though. With iTunes being the number one seller of all music, we have to just carve out our space as best we can. The funny thing J asked me before we signed our business loan papers was if we were attempting to sell lemonade at a time when everyone was buying bottled water. With some due diligence, we convinced ourselves that we could make a good run of this business and that we were not a Tower Records or Sam Goody's. With each day, our brand gains more recognition. We're just waiting for that to translate into the sales we need to continue to grow.

J says that he's already seeing some movement in product from our website, and our in-store sales are creeping upward at a snail's pace. I don't know how much of that is coming from my connection to *Soul Sista* or how much of it is coming from our other marketing efforts. But when you're a small business, and everything finally starts to move in a positive direction, you keep doing everything, rather than try to figure out whether its the sugar or the lemons bringing the new customers in.

"So how did it go?"

These are the words I am greeted by as I walk into C&J's Rare Grooves. J is grinning, his laptop open in front of him.

"Better than I expected."

"I need details. Break it down so that it will henceforth and forevermore be broke, my brotha," he says, closing his laptop and rubbing his hands together Mr. Miyagi-style.

"You know you can just wait for my post to go up this week," I respond, toying with him.

"Cool, after all of these years, you do me like *this*? Like I'm some Joe Blow off the street? Come on up off it now. I ain't reading shit that I can get firsthand."

I smile and take a seat behind the counter. I tell him about how Sarah looked in her black dress, about the dinner, and about our time at the cafe afterwards.

"Sounds like she has a lot of potential," he says. "Could this mean that you might actually go off the bachelor's market in the next decade? Inquiring minds want to know."

"I'm just taking it a date at a time. We'll see."

I glance at the clock on the wall. It's about five minutes before nine in the morning, so I go ahead and unlock the front door.

"So when are you gonna e-mail this blog entry to the magazine?" J asks, lifting up a box of t-shirts onto the counter and taking out a few to fold.

"Tomorrow."

"And when's your next date?"

"This Friday."

"What if you like this girl, too?"

" I don't know."

"I'd hate to be in your shoes," he says. " I like to create my own schedule. If I feel like having a woman over, then cool. But sometimes I don't want the stress of having to entertain. Shit, just give me a box of Kleenex and bottle of Jergens, and a brotha is good to go."

I laugh, as I grab a few shirts to fold. "Well, to each his own."

"I'm just saying," he says. "No need in making things too complicated."

"Well, while you're handling your business, just make sure you wash your hands before you handle our swag, dude."

"Fuck you very much, Cool. Fuck you very much."

9

———

Denise Mallory calls me shortly after receiving my e-mail.

"You're a pretty good storyteller. I really got into your date. I can tell you were feeling her."

"We had a good time, and I'll leave it at that," I say. "You know, it still feels funny writing all of this stuff down. It's like nothing is really sacred anymore."

"Well, I guess it just comes with the territory," she offers. "Are you looking forward to your next date?"

"I don't even know anymore. I feel like I should be going out with Sarah again—just to see if things click all the way around," I respond.

"I understand. You should definitely go out with her again after you do your other two dates."

So this is the price of free advertising, I tell myself. Part of me is curious about who the other women are, but there's Angie's voice in the back of my head whispering, "They're pimping you."

"Can I ask you something?" I say.

"Sure."

"Is this really what black women want to read about on your website? Some dude sorting through women in search of some magical relationship?"

"Well, we don't look at it that way."

I can tell that I have put her in a strange space, but there's a part of me that doesn't want to stop there. "Just so I'm clear, how does *Soul Sista* look at it?"

"It's all about possibilities, Cool," she says. "Women just want to know that romance is still alive, that men still care, that a bachelor like yourself could still be looking for the type of love that a good woman has to offer."

I don't say anything in response, mainly because I can't think of anything to say. She seems genuinely hurt by the inference that either I am a "man ho" or that her readers are desperate for entertainment, love, or both. The line has been drawn in the sand, and either I'm on board or I'm not.

"Hey, look, Cool. I'm sorry," she says, which surprises me.

"Sorry about what?"

"This. We did kind of dumped a lot of this stuff on you, and for someone reason I just assumed, you being a man and all, that you wouldn't have these types of existential dilemmas about the process."

I grin. "Are you mocking me?"

"Why? Do you feel mocked?"

I laugh, and when she joins me, I find myself dropping my guard. Maybe I *am* overthinking this a bit.

"So when do I need to check in with you again about the details of the next date?" I ask.

"I'll messenger over a packet to you this afternoon. And Cool?"

"Yes."

"I think you'll get a kick out of your next date?"

My eyebrow rises out of curiosity. "Is that a good thing or a bad thing?"

"Well, it's definitely not a bad thing."

8.

FACEBOOK IS A BITCH.

People you haven't seen or connected with since kindergarten pop out of thin air, sending friend requests. For the most part, it's been a decent experience, but with everyone flocking to the same social networking site, other problems can sometimes arise. And I can sense one of them arising right now as I log on to my profile page.

Waiting for me is a friendship request from Rhonda (yes, that Rhonda), the woman who took my heart out back and shot it like a wounded horse. Why the hell is she adding me? The last conversation I had with her was around the time she left me to handle the consequences of her infidelity. Now her friendship request is staring me, as Grace Jones said in *Boomerang*, "smack" in my face. The only thing missing is her repugnant purring.

I click on her name, linking me to her Facebook page. As soon as I get there, I quickly realize that I won't be able to see anything about her new life if I don't add her, because her entire profile is set to private. The only information available is her name. Even her profile picture is of some flower. In order to find out the basics about her (what she looks like now, where she is living, where she is working, if she's married and just chose not to change her surname, what her child looks like, and all of that other stuff that we claim to not care about when we break up with someone, but in actuality we do), I would have to click to accept her request. For a while I just stare at her name. Do I really want to open a rapport with her? Hadn't she done enough to mess up my life already?

I close up the laptop and walk into the kitchen. My refrigerator is nearly empty, save a jug of spring water, some leftover Chinese food from the other night, and a half-melted chocolate bar. In the adjacent freezer, I have a stack of TV meals. I reach for one of my shrimp creole dinners. I can hardly be bothered that the shrimp are just a hair bigger than sea monkeys. It's sustenance, and that's all that matters.

After slitting the film on the container and microwaving it twice (once and then shaking the loose ice around and reheating it again), I walk back and take a seat at my desk. I prop open the laptop again, and Rhonda's friend request is still right where I left it.

Seeing her name reminds me of the time that we went out to Stone Mountain to see the laser show. That night while driving back, listening to some old Maxwell songs, she nibbled on my earlobe, her tongue darting in and around my ear as she whispered what she was going to do to me when we pulled up to my apartment.

"I'm gonna fuck you so good," she cooed. "I'm getting wet just thinking about it."

She knew I loved it when she talked dirty. It

might not have been a natural fit for some women, but Rhonda definitely had a knack for making it work with me. I would spit it back at her, too.

"You gonna let me beat it out the frame, baby?"

She would smile when I tried to join in. "If you want to," she responded, running her tongue down my neck to the point that I could barely keep the steering wheel straight on the highway.

"You gonna kiss it for me, Cool," she moaned, her eyes half-closed and seductive.

"Yes," I say almost too quickly. "And you're gonna hook me up, too, baby?"

She smiled. "You know it."

She knew how to get me harder than an Upper East Side mortgage payment, and she always operated under the premise that if she got it up, she would put it down. And that night she put down some lovemaking on me that lives deep within my memories, even to this day. While I can't remember every time that we made love, that particular moment stands out among all the rest—even with my hating her like I do now.

And as I sit here reliving some of the best sex in my life, I find myself staring at the screen in both curiosity and horror at the fact that the screen is flashing an approval of her friendship request, my finger hovering sheepishly above the tracking pad as if it never betrayed me.

10

———

DATE TWO

TAYLOR

When I first moved to New York, my co-workers over at the investment bank would meet up Friday nights and head over to BBQs in the East Village, off of St. Mark. Ironically, we never ordered barbecue when we were there. We usually just ordered some Texas-sized frozen drinks and a large plate of fried chicken wings. The wings were just there so that we weren't drinking on an empty stomach. After that first drink, which we usually did with a shot of 151, we would have several more of them before leaving and heading up Amsterdam to a quaint little joint that played old school hip-hop, but was virtually empty. The drinks were cheap, though, and when we had done all of the drinking we had planned on doing, we'd walk a few doors down to another club, where the music was more contemporary and the girls were more plentiful. We did this nearly every Friday during my first year in the city.

As time went on, people changed jobs or moved away, and the crew fell apart. Without the comradery, BBQs just wasn't the same. Still from time to time I would think about those drinks and those chicken wings—and the fact that I had yet to order any barbecue from what was supposed to be a barbecue-centric restaurant.

I decided to put an end to that speculation and meet date number two at BBQs in the East Village. Sarah had spoiled me in terms of what I could expect on a first date, and most of that was because we had bypassed a lot of the customary first date games. With this new woman, Taylor, I wanted to dispense with pretense even faster than I had before. In my mind, ordering barbecue, something that was traditionally sloppy and forced you to eat with your thumbs sticking out, greasy with sauce, was a way of saying almost immediately that we weren't going to do that "cute" dining experience, where people hide behind their food. No, this was going to be a "cut to the chase" kind of date. I even set this one to start in the early afternoon and requested that she wear casual clothes that she already owned. (No point in going to Saks and dropping a grip on clothing in an effort to pretend like you just found your outfit lying in the back of the closet.) I wanted to meet the real person, not the facade that nearly every woman takes with her on that first date.

I had seen a picture of Taylor in the folder Denise sent over to me, but the picture didn't do her justice. She was cute in the photo, but now, standing in front of BBQ's, she looks beautiful in a way that is heightened even more by the sun reflecting off of her golden skin and curly Afro. She could easily be Esperanza Spalding's long lost twin.

We embrace as we introduce ourselves, and I am immediately struck by her sweet fragrance. It's subtle, but reminds me of candy. The scent makes me want to kiss her right there, but I settle on holding her hands in mine as I take in her glowing beauty.

She is dressed in a turquoise baby t-shirt with the words "funky chick" written across her breasts in white lowercase letters. Her skirt comes down to her calves and looks like a fabric that has simply been wrapped and tied around her waist. With her open-toed sandals, she has a very bohemian look.

"Very nice to meet you, Taylor," I say. "I'm really digging your flavor." I lower my gaze to her outfit.

She smiles and responds, "Thanks. Nice to meet you, too."

We walk in and are quickly ushered to a table by the window. The world of New York City moves outside, and sitting here feels like we are right next to a television, where the only channel is stuck on moving taxis, wandering students, and photograph-hungry tourists. But none of that matters as I sit across from Taylor.

"Interesting place for a first date, huh?" she says, lifting the menu.

"Ever been here before?"

"Can't say that I have. I don't eat out much."

We are interrupted by the server, who comes to take our drink orders.

"I'll have a water," Taylor says.

"Water?" I ask. "You sure you don't want something a bit more flavorful?"

"Water is just fine," she responds, ignoring my mild attempt at humor.

The server turns to me. "And you, sir?"

For a moment, I consider ordering water, just like Taylor, but as I open my mouth, I decide against ordering like my date again. Sarah had gotten that luxury, if that's what you could call it. I was going to order what I wanted. "I'll have a Texas sized pina colada with a shot of 151."

The server looks at me, his eyes questioning if I should be ordering liquor if my date isn't. I nod to him that my order is final, and he leaves the table.

"Do you drink?" I ask.

"No. I haven't had a drink since I was in college."

"What happened? You got picked up for a DUI or something?" I joke.

She smiles and shakes her head. "No, I just started meditating. That's all."

"So are you like a Buddhist or something?" I ask.

"Yes," she responds.

My mind drifts to the handful of things that I know about Buddhists, and it dawns on me that, unless she's monastic, she's not necessarily celibate, which would have been a potential deal-breaker. "Hold on. Are you a vegetarian?" I ask, realizing that I should have asked Denise a few more questions when I had her on the phone.

Somehow I am only mildly surprised when Taylor tells me, "Actually, I'm a raw food vegan."

This must've been what Denise was referring to when she hinted that my date would be interesting. I look at Taylor, wanting to kick myself. *And I thought that she got that glow from cocoa butter.*

"I am so sorry," I say. "We don't have to eat here, if you don't want to. I feel so stupid. With all of the chicken and pork in this place, I must be offending you in all kinds of ways."

"Don't sweat it. I'm not political about my food,

and I don't push my lifestyle on other people. You're not the first guy I've gone out with who likes to eat meat."

"Still," I say. "We can go somewhere and get a salad or something."

"I can get a salad here. I see it on the menu," she says pointing to a grilled chicken Caesar salad that would have to be stripped down completely to a pile of iceberg and romaine leaves to be vegan.

"I tell you what. Why don't we just get the drinks and then maybe you could take me to a restaurant that you enjoy eating at."

"Are you sure?"

"Yeah," I say, still shaking my head at how my plans for this date are backfiring.

"There is a dish I would love for you to try. It's a vegan chili!" she says, becoming more excited about the process of introducing me to something that's probably a beat away from being rabbit food.

"You said raw food though."

"It *is* raw food."

"So not only does it not have meat, but it's also cold?"

"I'll make a bet with you," she says. "If you don't like it, then I will stand on any corner in this city and sing a song for you."

"But can you sing?" I ask.

She looks at me, attempting to hold a straight face. "No."

"Well, I guess I'm in for a surprise either way then."

THE RESTAURANT IS CALLED "WE LIKE IT RAW," and although I understand the name, my thoughts revert back to sex. I look at Taylor and look away quickly. Too much, too soon, I tell myself.

We walk through the sparse population of people eating various raw concoctions. I had expected to see people who looked like they got off the last train from Berkeley, but what I see are ordinary New Yorkers having quiet meals. I could easily be walking into any Mom & Pop restaurant in the city.

I look at the menu posted on the wall behind the young lady at the register. Each of the combinations looks more horrifying than the next. Worst of all, I can feel no heat coming from the kitchen.

I see Taylor eyeing me cautiously. "You're still okay with this, right?"

I nod slowly. "Yeah."

"Want me to order for us? I think I can find a safe meal for your first raw vegan dish."

I inhale slowly, still baffled by the foods listed on the board. Pizza? Chili? Potato-less Potato Salad? I have to think hard on that last one, until I realize that you have to cook potatoes for a potato salad, so clearly they can't use actual potatoes in whatever they are calling a Potato-less Potato Salad. There are even chocolate chip cookies up there. Never have I conceived—in life—of a cookie that was not baked. Clearly, they must be talking about cookie dough and not actual cookies.

I look at Taylor and say, "Yeah. I think it would be best if you ordered."

She orders me the raw vegan chili, some of the Potato-less Potato Salad, a small side salad, a chocolate chip cookie, and a strawberry juice. I can't believe that she actually puts together a meal for me so quickly. Either she knows something that I don't or she's about to really push this date into the direction of "not gonna be pretty" territory. She orders herself a bowl of chili, some kind of grounded nut concoction, a side of the Potato-less Potato Salad, and a cookie.

"No salad for you!" I say, attempting to mimic the Soup Nazi from *Seinfeld*.

"Not this time," she says, smiling.

When we get our dishes, all served on what looks like recycled paper plates and bowls, I see her bow her head. I don't know what to do, so I just wait patiently for her to finish. When she does, I pick up my spoon and cautiously approach the chili. It looks like chili, but because I know there are no beans (which would have to be cooked), no meat, and no heat, I am preparing myself for the worse.

Rather than start her food, Taylor waits patiently for me to take my first bite. I suddenly become acutely aware of the journey of this first spoonful of chili from the bowl to my mouth. As I eye the spoon moving closer, almost like someone else is serving me, my mind flashes to an image of Taylor standing on some arbitrary corner singing her heart out for me, off-key and all. I part my lips and brace myself for the first bite. When it hits my tongue, the flavors spread out and I start to chew. Outside of it being room temperature, it actually tastes pretty good. There's even the texture of meat in there from something. I look at the bowl and suddenly realize that I can polish it off with no problem.

"What do you think?" she asks.

"Not bad at all."

She nods, chuckling.

"What's so funny?"

"I'm so glad that you didn't make me sing. That would've been really embarrassing."

I laugh with her, as she begins to eat.

The Potato-less Potato Salad is all right, but nothing to write home about. It actually tastes more like bitter apples posing as potatoes, beneath this mayonnaise-type flavoring. Up until now, I haven't even considered why the French would refer to potatoes as apples of the earth. They must have eaten this stuff, apparently.

Ordering the salad was definitely a safe move and a solid palate cleanser. But my mind is already racing ahead to that final piece of food on my tray: the chocolate chip cookie. I figure this is the deal-breaker right here for whether or not this meal will come together.

"It won't bite," Taylor says, nodding at my cookie.

"How can you have a cookie when you don't bake it?" I muse, lifting it from the small plate.

It feels like a ball of firm dough between my fingertips, and I playfully wonder if it's safe to eat. I bite in and begin to chew. As the taste of sweet cocoa spreads across my tongue, I realize that I'm actually eating a *real* dessert.

"How do they get it this sweet? Is there refined sugar in here?"

"No," she responds. "It's agave nectar. Sweeter than sugar, but natural."

"It's not bad. It doesn't feel like a cookie when I touch it, but it definitely tastes like one," I say.

"So," she says, as we clean our plates, "how was your first raw vegan meal?"

"I kind of dug it," I respond. "But I won't lie to you. I'll probably be craving a steak later on though."

"Fair enough," she says, as we empty our plates into the recycle bin by the door.

❦

AFTER OUR MEAL, WE WALK AROUND THE VILLAGE and eventually wind up at Washington Square Park, where we grab a bench across the street from NYU.

Students walk back and forth, their backpacks and computer bags draped across their shoulders. A group of older guys, possibly veterans, huddle over a chessboard, and off to the side, a group of tourists are photographing the various activity around them. I look over at the arch where two statues of George Washington stand across from each other, framing the entrance. 5th Avenue dead-ends into the park, and across the street are some very expensive-looking row houses, nearly identical to the ones in Will Smith's movie *I Am Legend*. I look back at Taylor who is also taking in our surroundings.

"Can I ask you a question?" I start.

"Sure."

"Why did you agree to do this date?"

She watches the students moving aimlessly about the sidewalk. "Why not?"

"So is this like a bucket list item for you?"

"No," she chuckles. "I don't have a bucket list. I just do what I feel compelled to do. I saw your picture on the website, and I thought to myself, 'He might be a fun person to hang out with.'"

"I see," I say, looking at her crossed legs, one of her sandals falling away from her heel. "So you're not really looking for anything serious then?"

"Serious is a matter of perception. Let's just enjoy the moment for what it is. If it leads to more, we'll follow it there."

"Okay," I offer, but I realize that I have no idea of what that would mean if she ended up being the woman I selected from this process.

She turns to face me, her smooth leg brushing against my khakis. "I know you had a good time on your last date. I can tell she struck a chord with you."

Damn, I think to myself. That's definitely one of the downsides of this entire thing being blogged about on the *Soul Sista* site. No telling what my third date will think of me by the time she reads through the accounts of my other two dates.

"We had a good time," I offer, hoping to neutralize any further discussion of Sarah.

"So are you having a good time now?" she asks.

"Definitely. I don't think I've felt healthier in my life."

She laughs, and as her body bounces, her curly Afro jiggles. The gesture is very charming, and I want to reach over and touch her hand, but I don't feel an opening just yet.

"So tell me a little bit about yourself," she says.

"I'm from Mississippi, but I went to school in Atlanta. Fell in love. Got my heart broken. Moved to New York to work on Wall Street. Now I own half of a record store in Harlem."

"God, Cool! You know how to suck the life out of a story, don't you?" she jokes.

"Well, that's pretty much been my life so far."

"So you define yourself by what has happened to you, not by who you are?"

I know the question isn't meant to be a heavy one, but it feels like it. I sense I'm getting judged on a level, and that makes me feel a bit uncomfortable, as if I am not a complete person. The sad thing is that I start to wonder if she's right.

"I think I have a good idea of who I am," I say, careful to project confidence this time.

"So tell me."

"I'm a good man who wants to do the right thing. I love music more than anything in the world. In fact, I believe there's no ill that can't be cured by Earth, Wind & Fire or Stevie Wonder. I believe in the possibility of love—even after all of the shit that I've been through. Someone once told me that there's someone for everyone, and I guess I've always questioned if somehow I might've been the one exception to that rule. This experience is definitely a new one for me, so I'm just trying to see where it goes." When I finish I do a fake wipe of my brow and ask, "What about you? Who are you?"

"Didn't you read my t-shirt," she says. "I'm a funky chick!"

"I see," I say, admiring her dimples.

"I'm a simple girl who grew up in South Jersey. I don't really care a lot for labels. I love music, and I think that Minnie Riperton and Nina Simone are the closest things to angels to ever walk the earth. I love art—I sketch and write poetry. I believe very much in love and in living in the now. I love smelling the roses, not just admiring them from a distance. I don't know. I guess I'm just an open person like that."

"Really?" I respond. "When you say that you don't care for labels, what do you mean? Clothes? Titles?"

"All of it. To label someone is to confine them to being just that one thing. I don't like labels in any area of my life."

Now I am curious, so I ask, "So you don't believe in labels like girlfriends and boyfriends, husbands and wives?"

"Don't get me wrong. I do believe in commitment, but I have noticed that people behave differently when labels are involved. I like just being with someone because I want to, not because I feel obligated to."

As I listen to her, the truth of her words has a calming effect over me.

"So," I say. "What would you like to do next?"

"I'm good just being with you."

She smiles, her lips curving upward sweetly. I find myself unable to do anything but smile along with her.

"I can dig that, Funky Chick."

11

———

Writing about Taylor proves to be more difficult than I expected. I haven't been around a woman in a long time who's taught me so much in just an afternoon. I am so intrigued by her mind that it almost overpowers her beauty. When she speaks, she brings up things that force me to think differently. I don't know how much of that is her being Buddhist, being vegan, or just being herself.

With Sarah, there was the playful banter, the flirting, the sexual energy. But with Taylor, our date was about the mind and the soul. They are definitely two very different women, and to compare the two dates would be like comparing night and day. I haven't spoken to either of them since those first dates, and I'm trying to wait on doing so until after this third date with a woman named Roxanne.

Although it takes me a while to draft my blog entry, I finish shortly after ten in the evening and email it to Denise at *Soul Sista*.

At this point, I can honestly say that I have no clue how any of this will end up.

MY VERY FIRST GIRLFRIEND *EVER* DUMPED ME less than three hours after she checked the "yes" box. Her name was Brenda Williams, and she was a skinny third grader who wore thick glasses. Even back then I was scouting potential, trying to see what other guys couldn't see. She was pretty much invisible to the other kids because she was always off to herself, reading books.

One day, while we were taking a spelling test, I saw her take off her glasses and wipe her eyes. In the seconds before she put them back on, I saw a girl who had it going on. She was smart *and* pretty, and immediately I knew that combination would work for me going forward.

I worked on my first love letter during recess, and I put so much time into printing each word clearly and neatly that my hand nearly cramped. I went after Brenda with everything in my arsenal. At the end of the letter I drew three boxes and asked her to check one: "YES," "NO," or "MAYBE SO."

I dropped the letter onto her desk right before Social Studies that afternoon. Because I sat across the room from her, I had to sweat out the rest of the period to see if she would respond before we went to our Phys Ed class.

When the bell rang, I sat at my desk, fiddling with my things so that I could give her time to walk past me. She came up beside my desk and dropped the letter back onto my backpack and walked away. I waited until everyone had almost cleared out of Mrs. Jamison's class before I stood and grabbed my things. I floated slowly behind my class as we headed toward the gym.

While we waited in a line outside the gym entrance, I opened the letter. It was the same one that I had written, but the YES box had been checked!

At that moment, I felt as though I would bust out of my skin and soar up into the sky. Even during Phys Ed, I watched her and would smile at her whenever our eyes met. I had my first girlfriend, and life couldn't have been sweeter.

By the end of the school day, while I stood around with my boys waiting on the bus, one of them, Joe Lee, leaned over and said to me, "They say you liking Brenda now. Whatchu want with that four-eyed girl, man? Them glasses so thick they got x-ray vision."

The insults caught me off guard. I had never thought about what other people would say about Brenda being my girl.

Then my friend Nate joined in. "Yeah, man. She got a kitchen on the back of her neck, too. If you go to run your fingers through them naps, you'll get cut up."

They began to laugh, and, to not feel so out of place, I laughed, too.

That's when I heard a soft voice behind me. "Chauncey." The voice was so weak and timid that I almost didn't hear it over our laughter. In fact, it was only when I saw the expressions on Joe Lee's and Nate's faces that I knew who was standing behind me.

I turned around slowly, bracing myself.

"Chauncey," Brenda said, her eyes moist, "I'm not your girlfriend anymore."

And with that, she walked away and left me standing there with the two knuckleheads who had caused all of my problems.

For years I blamed Joe Lee and Nate, but it wasn't until I got to high school that I realized I had fucked that situation up myself. I had not stood up for her, and even worse, I had put someone else's opinions above my own. I liked her, and that was all that mattered, not anything that Joe Lee or Nate had to say about it.

Even now that I'm thirty, I swear that philosophy still holds true—but I can't help seeing the irony in dating women selected for me by other people. I guess as long as I'm true to myself, then just maybe I can redeem myself for letting Brenda go so easily.

I DECIDE NOT TO READ THE BLOG ENTRY I wrote on Taylor when it posts. Instead I try to stay focused on the sliver of information that Denise has spent money having delivered to the store. I know nothing about this next girl at all, except for the fact that she's in "entertainment" (whatever that means) and that her name is Roxanne. Her picture is a black and white headshot, and while she looks dolled up and pretty, I learned from Taylor that pictures don't always tell the whole story. There is definitely not enough information in the packet to justify Denise using a messenger to send it. If we were talking about top secret plans for nuclear warheads, that would be a different story. One thing is for sure: if J and I did any of this foolishness of using a messenger for little shit like this, we'd be out of business by the end of the month.

After J finishes ringing up a customer, he takes a seat on the stool next to mine.

"Cool, we might just make it into the black sooner than later."

The comment is refreshing, since it feels like we have been losing money for so long that raw fear has set in.

"Yeah," I say, acting as if all of this is by design. "I see even Ray-Ray is more motivated."

We watch Ray-Ray over against the back wall telling a group of young ladies about the electronic soul band J*Davey. Even the way he describes the music is more enthusiastic than normal. "Oh my god, these two are so nice! The sista, Jack Davey, sounds like what you would have if Prince and T-Boz had an illegitimate star child from Saturn—but in a good way!" The girls laugh and pick up the CD and a few t-shirts.

When they make it to the register, one of them points at the other and says, "I told you that was him."

They never speak to me directly, but they giggle about their experience in the store, and better still, they walk out having dropped about forty dollars apiece.

J turns to face me, as Ray-Ray joins us at the counter. "This *Soul Sista* thing is really good for us right now. You know how many online orders I had to fulfill this week? We're gonna have to place another order for t-shirts pretty soon. I even got a call from a small business journal about doing an interview with us. Word is really getting around that we're the spot to hit these days."

"Dude, that's crazy! Seems like all of this stuff just came out of left field. I just hope we can keep it up," I say.

"Yo," Ray-Ray says, "I heard some sistas on the subway talking about who you need to pick as your girl. One chick was like it was a no-brainer. You had to go with that Sarah girl. They said that dark skinned sistas don't get enough love, and if you picked that yella girl over the darker sister, then you must be color struck."

I shrug. "I guess a woman's personality really doesn't matter much anymore." My comment is supposed to read as sarcastic, but Ray-Ray's dumb ass is nodding as if I've just spoken some kind of truth.

J places a hand on my shoulder. "But the sistas out there will be checking to see who you pick, so just make sure you stay true to whatever rubric you're using."

"Rubric? This isn't a formula or anything. These are real women, and this is real life."

"Spoken like a true reality show star," J says, laughing.

Ray-Ray says, "I'm just sayin' you will have some haters out there if you go with Golden 'Fro."

"I'll tell you what, everybody," I start. "Let me handle the women, and you guys handle keeping us solvent in the meantime."

J nods and returns to his laptop. Ray-Ray shrugs his shoulders and walks over to a stack of CDs and starts to organize them.

I swear these days I feel like everyone must think I'm just one-dimensional. For the first time since all of this started, I feel like I need a break.

12

"Don't bounce him like that, Cool. He'll spit up on you," Angie says as she walks over to sit next to Aaron and me. "He just ate. Take this." She hands me a towel to drape over my shoulder.

"Awww, doesn't he looks so handsome with his big cousin!" Tracy says, leaning forward on the recliner across the room.

I pull Aaron closer so that he is right in the nook of my neck.

"There he goes," Angie says, laughing.

I look at my shoulder and see white spit-up running down my t-shirt.

"Guess you should have put the rag on your other shoulder," Angie volunteers.

"Obviously," I respond, my face beginning to twitch involuntarily from the smell.

I hand Aaron back to Angie and start to wipe at the white cream-like substance with the rag.

"You might want to put some soap and water on that before it dries in there and you wind up smelling like breast milk for the rest of the day," Tracy offers.

"Yeah, that definitely sounds like a plan."

I dart to the bathroom down the hall and quickly remove my shirt, running soap and water over it, before ringing it out.

"Hey, Angie!" I call out. "You have one of those C&J t-shirts I gave you a while back?"

"Yeah, I'll get it for you," she responds from the den.

I'm so thankful my cousin wears her clothing oversized. In fact, sometimes I joke with her about how her wardrobe is better than my own. She laughs and just responds that she loves the feeling of being free in clothes that have room. She even made me promise that when she died I wouldn't let Tracy or her mother put her in a dress before they put her in the ground.

"Here you go," she says, tossing a navy blue t-shirt at me. I'm pleasantly surprised to see that it's actually been worn and washed.

"You've been out there reppin' for us?" I ask.

"You know how we do it, cuz!" she says, walking back to the den.

"Hey, Angie, you know you're the shit, right?" Just then I realize that Aaron is in the other room. "My bad! I mean you're the bomb."

I hear both Angie and Tracy laughing. Even with Aaron's gurgling, he sounds like he's in on the joke, too.

I walk back into the den. Tracy and Angie are curled up on the couch, and I have to admit that they complement each other well visually. Angie with her thick, short frame, her skin the color of bronze, and Tracy with the dreadlocks, slight frame, and reddish complexion. Aaron, with his light complexion, looks like a little light bulb between the two of them.

I laugh and poke fun at them. "How are the two of you gonna have a kid the color of Al B. Sure?"

"Cool," Angie laughs, "We ain't fooling nobody here. That kid ain't supposed to look like me!"

"Yeah, but he looks like his daddy was of the Caucasian persuasion."

"Unh unh," Tracy says, "Aaron is one hundred percent Zulu-Masai stock."

"Okay, Miss School Daze. Whatever you want to believe."

Tracy pipes up. "You have to look at his ears. That's the color he's gonna change to."

I look at Aaron. "You hear that little cuz? They think you're Zartan from G.I. Joe. Just put you out in the sun and you'll change colors."

Aaron giggles when I say this, but I know he's only responding to my facial expression.

"So," Angie says, adjusting herself on the couch so that Aaron rests more comfortably against her arm, "I've been reading about your exploits online. Sounds like you have quite the decision to make."

I lift my head and exhale. "This process is crazy. And I still have one more woman to go out with."

"I'd hate to be you," Angie says and then adds, "well maybe not."

Tracy pops her on her leg, and Angie laughs.

"It'll all work out," I say, hoping to change subjects. "Ain't that right, little cuz?" This time Aaron looks away from me to the *Backyardigans* playing in the background on the flatscreen. He has clearly lost interest in the grown folks' conversation.

"You can't talk to him when Austin's on the screen," Tracy says.

Angie nods, kissing Aaron on his head. "Cool, I wanted to ask you something?"

"Okay," I respond, unsure of whether I'm going to get another "you're being pimped" speech.

"I've been talking to Tracy about this, and I just wanted to run it by you." Her face becomes serious, and my curiosity is immediately piqued.

She continues. "I want to go home to see Mama—and I want to take Tracy and Aaron with me."

I nod slowly, wondering what has brought this on. "Why now?"

"You know Mama had that scare with her blood sugar last year, and I don't know. I guess I've just been thinking that we need to get square with each other. If something happened to her with us being like this, I don't know how I could live that down."

"Aunt Jonetta doesn't hate you, you know."

"Yeah. I know."

"She'll have to accept you if she truly loves you."

"That's what I'm hoping, but the last time I went home, she spent the whole time trying to get me to go to church with her so her pastor could put his hands on me and cast the sin out of my body."

Normally, if Angie had said something like this, it would be tinged in humor, but today the words are just heavy. Now I'm concerned about her and her plan. "You sure you're ready to go through with this?"

She laughs. "Nope."

Tracy places a hand on Angie's shoulder.

"You know what?" I say. "Whatever happens when you get to Alabama, just know that I'm always on your side. After all, you can only do what you can do. No one can fault you for trying to build a bridge with Aaron's grandmother."

Angie nods and turns to face Tracy. "See," she says. "I told you my cousin was the shit."

I lower my eyes to Aaron, and Angie smiles, pointing to the television. "Don't worry. Austin's on right now."

13

———

Rhonda looks even better than she did when we first dated. I had held off on going to her Facebook page, but now that I scan through her photos, assuming that they are current, I find myself remembering all of the wonderful moments we shared before the incident that caused our break-up. This is why I hate looking at pictures of her. I end up romanticizing the past far too much.

One of her photo albums is called "My Treasure!!!" and the first picture I see is of a beautiful little girl with braided and beaded hair. She looks like a miniature version of Rhonda. I click open the album, and there are several shots of this little girl smiling and posing in various environments. One of the pictures has Rhonda and Treasure standing side by side, holding each other. I find myself unable to keep from smiling. I had often wondered whether I would ever want to see the child who was at the heart of our breakup, but now that I have, I feel a sense of peace. Rhonda just looks so happy standing there. Incidentally, there is no guy in any of the pictures, which is not surprising since Rhonda's status is listed as "single."

I want to hate her all over again, but I can't bring myself to go there, not with Treasure staring through the screen at me. One thing I notice (and am immediately thankful for) is that the little girl doesn't seem to have any features of her father. I think if Treasure looked like a blend of two people as opposed to the spitting image of one, I would have a much harder time with this. As I look back and forth between them, I wonder what Treasure would have looked like if I had been her father. Would she still look like a clone of her mother, or would she have something of mine? My ears? My nose? My eyes?

Rhonda has not messaged me directly since I accepted her request, but I have noticed that she has clicked "Like" for a few of my comments. I guess that's as safe a way as any to ease into a conversation with a person. Still, I don't know what I would say if we ever did speak to each other. How do you pick up from such a bad breakup?

"How are you doing?" she might ask, and I would be forced to respond, "Not bad, considering the devastating heartbreak you laid on me nine years ago."

Surely I'm beyond that. At least I hope.

Maybe she read *Soul Sista* and has been following the blog. She could have just told me what she wanted from me when she sent the friendship request rather than have me sitting here guessing about what to expect next from her.

I'm probably overthinking this, I know. Maybe it's all just innocent, but it seems these days that I am more popular than I care to be. I guess that would make most anyone more paranoid of people's intentions.

Soon enough all of this hoopla with *Soul Sista* will be behind me. Hopefully by that time, C&J's Rare Grooves will be all the better for it. And maybe —just maybe—there will be a woman standing by my side once the storm has passed.

14

DATE THREE

ROXANNE

One of my favorite movies when I was growing up was *Strictly Business*, that flick with Tommy Davidson and that dude from the *Cosby Show*. More importantly, it was the movie that presented Halle Berry to the world as "Natalie," the 90's version of the video vixen.

I guess one of the things that appealed to me the most about the movie was that the nerdy guy became cool and got the girl. How contrived the plot was and how rushed the sequence of events was didn't matter to me. All that mattered was that a square, like me, could wind up with the pretty girl.

Growing up, I had arms like pipe cleaners and weighed barely a buck soaked and wet. It took years and a lot of milk and exercising to get to my current physique. I was never the fastest kid on the playground or the strongest person at the gym, but for some reason I took to school like a fish to water. The only thing about high school was that the better I did in the classroom, the lamer I was to everyone else. It wasn't until I got to Morehouse that being the bookish type of brother proved to be to my advantage. And by that time, there were hundreds of Natalies throughout the Atlanta University Center vying for attention. The only thing that was missing was the multimillion-dollar Savoy Towers deal to save the day.

All of this rushes to the front of my mind as soon as I set eyes on Roxanne, my third and final date. We're standing in front of a swanky little restaurant that caters to the local Harlem buppie population, and she's wearing a hot red dress, her long hair falling in curls onto her shoulders. Her body is bodacious in a way that seems almost exaggerated. I feel strange standing next to her. It feels as if she's a three-dimensional super heroine and I am just a mere mortal. For some strange reason, I sense she would be the woman drawn to a professional athlete and not a fledgling entrepreneur like myself.

As we shake hands, I find my eyes unable to avoid spying her legs and hips, her small waist and flat stomach, and of course those voluptuous breasts. Her caramel skin and cat-like eyes add to the exotic allure of her aura. To put it bluntly, she looks like a video vixen. She's the quintessential Natalie, more than Halle ever was.

As we take our seats in the back of the restaurant, I try to push all of this out of my mind. Roxanne deserves a fair shake, just like Sarah and Taylor.

There's still some sunlight outside, and the clock on the wall reads seven-fifteen. It could be that the extra lighting makes her make-up even more pronounced.

"I been waiting forever to get with you," she starts.

"Oh really?" I answer. "Why's that?"

"I'm not trying to diss these other chicks, but I knew when I seen you that we was supposed to be together. And I got up this morning and read my horoscope, and you know what it had said?"

"No," I answer, still unable to shake the "I seen you" part of her comment.

"It had said that my life was about to change for the better."

"For real?" I say, glancing around the room. There must be a camera in here somewhere, although I figure I'm way too common to be "punk'd."

"Whatchu looking for?" she asks.

"Oh, I thought I heard someone call my name. That's all."

"Oh, okay," she says, glancing at her fingernails. "Sometimes I be thinking that someone is calling my name and it ain't nobody. But one day, I won't be able to go nowhere without folks being like, 'That's Roxanne! Heyyyyy!'"

I nod. I am momentarily at a loss for words. Finally, I say, "So you want to be famous?"

"Well, I'm already a actress, small roles right now though. I also did a few videos. So I guess I'm kinda famous already, but I really want to be more famous. Know what I mean?"

"Okay," is all I can muster. "So what made you want to go on this date?"

"It's like you was a cutie already, but I know this is also like reality television, too, except there ain't no television. I figure it could be like knocking out two birds with one stone."

One of my eyebrows arches involuntarily. "So you're more concerned about me writing about you than you are about trying to make a connection with me?"

Sensing that things are going south, I see her shift uncomfortably in her chair. "Naw," she says. "I'm really feelin' you. I'm just the kind of chick that's straight up. I'm direct. I speak my mind."

"So what do you want to see happen tonight?"

"I figure we could get something to eat—and talk, you know? And if you feel like it, we could go back to my place and see how things go from there."

While I had considered the possibility of one of my dates wanting to get intimate on our first date, I never could have predicted the bluntness that Roxanne was putting on the table right now.

"Why don't we just take everything a step at a time?"

She smiles weakly. "Yeah, that's what I meant, you know? Let's just see how it goes. But know that I'm already feeling you, so it's more on you than it is on me."

We order. This time I order a seafood cioppino, a tomato-based stew of shellfish, shrimp, and calamari poured over a bed of linguine. Roxanne orders a filet mignon and a lobster tail. Yes, tonight we will actually exhaust the per diem given to me by *Soul Sista*.

"So tell me about your store?" she says, sipping on a glass of chilled white zinfandel.

"We've been opened for almost a year—up here in Harlem. Our store is called C&J's Rare Grooves, and we specialize in carrying soul artists, particularly smaller acts and indies."

"Like who?" she asks.

"Carmen Rogers, Conya Doss, Eric Roberson, The Foreign Exchange, Donnie, The Fuzz Band,

Georgia Anne Muldrow, Jimmie Reign. The list goes on and on. You ever heard of any of them?"

She shakes her head and then stops. "Hold up. Did you say Foreign Exchange? Ain't that the group that did that song with that girl?" She starts humming the song, and her voice is in pitch-perfect.

"You're talking about 'Sincere' with YahZarah? Yeah, that's them."

She starts smiling. "That song is hot! I heard it at one of my girl's cribs and asked her to make me CD. I just don't be knowing who these people are, but I know the songs when I hear them."

I look at her, nodding. "I could put together a list of people for you to check out. Hey, you can even come by the store, and I'd be happy to play some of their music for you."

She takes another swallow of her zinfandel. "That's what's up."

"So who do you like to listen to?" I ask.

"I don't know," she says. "A little bit of everybody."

I lean forward, urging her to give me a few names.

"I don't know," she says again. "Raphael Saadiq, D'Angelo, Lalah Hathaway, India.Arie, Raheem De-Vaughn. You know, those kind of people."

I can feel the awkwardness from earlier lifting. "You ever been to the Capital City Jazz Fest in Columbia, Maryland? They have one every June."

"Are you serious? I been to the last three. Me and my girls go every year."

I am now visibly smiling. "So I guess we could have met before. I've been going for the past five years."

She starts chuckling. "Well," she says, "when I go, I don't be dressed like this."

"What does that mean?" I ask.

"I be going to kick back when I go there, so I ain't dressing like I'm going on a date. We just be rocking jeans and baby tees—and baseball caps," she adds. "You can't get loose when you all did up."

Now as I look at her, I realize that there's much more to Roxanne than the exterior she's presenting to me right now. From the sounds of it, she might actually be my musical soul mate. Still seeing her looking like a cover model for *King* magazine is straining my ability to make the connection to who she really is.

"You know, you didn't have to get dressed up for this date. We could have kept this really laid back."

She smiles, and this time I look beneath her make-up and hair, and I see a sista who is naturally beautiful, but somewhere along the way she realized that she could doll herself out to get much more attention.

"I wanted to make sure that if anyone saw us together, they knew how we did it," she says.

"I see. Well, let me tell you something," I say, my tone softening. "What we do is not about what other people think. This is *our* time. Our chance to get to know each other. Don't worry about people checking for us. I don't live my life that way. I just want us to have a good time."

She looks confused for a moment. "So you woulda rather gone out with the Capital Jazz Fest me?"

"No," I answer. "I would've rather gone out with the real you."

She holds up her empty glass, and a server appears to refill it. She looks down into the glass, seemingly distraught.

"What's wrong?" I ask.

"I'm blowing it, right?" she asks, and I am taken aback. This is the most vulnerable she's appeared all night.

"No, you're not blowing it," I say. "In fact, I think you're a pretty chill woman."

She lifts her head slowly, attempting to hide her smile.

When our dishes finally arrive, I spend the rest of dinner talking to Rochelle Nichols, not the facade of Roxanne.

WE DON'T LEAVE THE RESTAURANT UNTIL JUST after nine. Rochelle stops walking and places a hand on my shoulder. "Give me a moment," she says. "These shoes! Ooh. I don't know if I can keep walking in these things."

We haven't walked more than a block. I look at the sidewalk and realize that we'll have to flag a cab, because I wouldn't wish walking barefoot on this dirty ass New York sidewalk on my worst enemy.

"Okay," I say, placing my hand around her waist and moving us back out of the way of pedestrian traffic. Her body is soft, in an alluring way. The irony is that she might've looked unreal before, but she feels one hundred percent real now. "Where would you like to go? I'll get us a cab."

She exhales as she considers this. "We can go back to my place so I can change."

I don't know if this is an extension of her bedroom invitation from earlier, but the strain in her face seems real—and we obviously won't be getting very far down any street in this city if her feet are hurting.

"Okay," I respond.

I escort her to the corner and hail down the next cab. As we take our seats in the back, the cab driver asks, "So where to?"

I look at Rochelle. She looks at me without saying a word. Then she turns to face the driver. "Flatbush Avenue," she says.

Damn, I think to myself.

We're headed all the way to Brooklyn.

DON'T GET ME WRONG. I LOVE BROOKLYN.

I love the people, the neighborhoods, the flavor. But I live in Harlem, USA, which is almost like another planet. To get to Brooklyn, you have to drive down the BQE or head towards City Hall and take the Brooklyn Bridge across. To put it plainly, we are taking a trek, and when you factor that we are in a cab, that constitutes a trip.

As we speed along in the cab, cutting back and forth between other traffic, I realize that the chances of my getting out of Brooklyn and back to Harlem tonight are slim to none. There just aren't enough cabs running the distance back and forth between the two places at night. Factor in that we're dealing with two gentrified neighborhoods known primarily for their high black populations (although the white populations are steadily increasing), and my options for getting home tonight rest solely on my ability to hail a gypsy cab or wait indefinitely for the subway to come through. Or, and I am trying not to focus on this option, I can just wait and catch a cab the next day when the sun rises.

We pull up to an old brownstone apartment building, and I pay the driver. A few of the guys on the block start speaking to Rochelle immediately.

"Damn, shorty! You look so good I'd drank yo bathwater with a crazy straw!" one guy says.

Another one says, "I'd suck yo toes!"

I look at Rochelle, and she only smiles, so I brush off the comments. No need in defending her honor if it's not being insulted.

I place my hand on the small of her back and escort her through the gate in front of the building, and for a moment I feel like I'm replaying Kid's date with the "around the way" girl from the movie *Class Act*.

A guy calls out from behind me. "Man, I'd rob a bank to be you tonight!"

I don't bother looking back.

She unlocks the door, and I walk in behind her. We take the stairs to the second floor, and as she sways her sexy ass just inches from my face, I realize that I'm more drawn to her than I would've admitted earlier. Before she opens the door, she turns to me and says, "You'll have to excuse my mess. I didn't expect to be coming back here with a man, so don't trip if you see things laying around."

"Well, okay," I respond, not sure what to make of her comment, given her earlier invitation for me to come back here and apparently see her place like this.

As soon as she opens the door, I immediately understand her warning. There are things everywhere. No food or anything else, for that matter, decomposing on the coffee table or the floor, but there are dresses and shirts on plastic hangers dangling from half-opened doors. Clearly, she must buy clothes that can't be placed in a dryer. In addition, every other doorknob has a purse hanging from it. The main area of her apartment simply looks like the inside of anyone else's closet.

On a table across the room is a small pile of hair, which she notices immediately and runs to grab and tuck under her arm before going into her room. "I'll be right back," she says, trotting across the floor, her shoes coupled with her purse beneath her other arm.

There is a couch facing a thirty-two inch flat screen television. I take a seat in the center so that I don't lean on any of the garments she has stretched out over the arms. Picking up the remote control, I flip on the power and scan channels aimlessly until I hear her reappear behind me.

"See anything you like?" she asks.

I start to say, "no," but I look away from the television and at her in her jeans and snug wife-beater, a simple relaxed-fit baseball cap atop her head. "Well, you're looking casually fly."

"Thank you," she responds. "Let me move some of this stuff. You know, I just wasn't expecting no company."

She walks around the couch grabbing stray clothes, and when her arms begin to fill up, I ask if she needs any help. "No, I got it," she says, toting her load into her bedroom where I assume she is dumping the pile into another pile.

She returns, cascading barefoot across the floor, and I have to admit that she is very cute in her mannerisms. She takes a seat on the couch next to me.

"Kick 'em up," I tell her, pointing to her feet.

"Oh, I can't let you do that."

"You've been complaining about your feet for a while now. Prop them up here. I won't take no for an answer."

She smiles and backs into the other arm of the couch, placing her feet onto my lap. I am not a foot man like J, but I feel this is the least I can do for her since clearly she's been trying all night, in her own way, to make a positive impression on me.

Her feet are warm, and I begin to carefully knead the balls of her feet and massage the arches.

"Lord have mercy," she whispers under her breath. "That feels incredible."

I nod. "So tell me about what you do for a living, or are you one hundred percent an actress—like you said earlier."

She closes her eyes, enjoying her foot massage. "Acting is one of the craziest jobs out there, because everything is just a gig. You milk it while you can, and when it's over, you gotta go and get a whole new job. So when I ain't working, I work at this cafe over in Forte Green. It's pretty cool. I get to meet famous people there sometimes, too. Spike Lee be up in there a lot."

"Did you always want to be an actress?" I ask.

"Ever since I can remember. I was always trying to get up in front of somebody and do my thing." She exhales deeply, her eyes closed. "So what about you? You always want to have your own store?"

I continue to rub up her ankles and onto her

lower leg, through her jeans. "If you would have told me when I was little that I would own a record store in New York City, I would have told you that you were crazier than a pig tap dancing in the pulpit of First Baptist Church. I mean, I wanted to own a business, but a record store? Hell no."

"Damn, Cool. That's some pretty country shit to say. Where you from?"

"Oh," I say, chuckling. "I grew up in Mississippi."

"I got folks down there. You know the LeBoufs?"

I look at her incredulously, but her eyes are still closed. "You'll have to tell me what town, because Mississippi is a state." Normally, I give people hell when they do this, but I don't want to interrupt the evening with unnecessary stuff.

"Right. I think they from around Jackson."

I am convinced that most people think that Mississippi only has one city: Jackson. So to them everything is around Jackson. That's just a shortcut for saying that they really think that Mississippi is just some giant city. I don't know if Rochelle is talking about the real "around Jackson" (Pearl, Clinton, Brandon, Ridgeland, Flowood, Madison, Canton, etc.) or if she's just making a generic reference. Being from Corinth, which is as far north as you can get in Mississippi—and at least four hours from the Jackson metro area—I have heard it all.

To politely move forward, I tell her that I don't know any LeBoufs and pray like hell that she doesn't ask me to deliver a message to these people when I go home for the holidays.

"That feels good on my legs," she says.

As my hands rest below her right knee, I realize

that it might've been better had she put on shorts. Her jeans are very tight, and I am having more difficultly gripping her body than I thought I would.

"You got anything that's a little looser to wear? I can't really get at your muscles," I say.

She opens her eyes and looks at me, as if checking to see if I am fucking with her or if I'm serious about what I am doing.

"I can just take them off," she says.

I'm at a loss for words. I probably should've considered that as an option to begin with, but knowing that I have to write about this date, I didn't want to do anything that wouldn't play well with the people over at *Soul Sista*. So I say the dumbest thing that I've said in quite some time: "Are you sure?"

"I'm not the kind of person to be embarrassed about my body. Not anymore."

"Not anymore?" I ask.

"I always been a thick sister, and even when all the boys wanted them skinny ass girls, I knew I was fine. My mama is thick, and she is beautiful. I took after my mama, so that mean I don't need nobody to tell me I ain't beautiful, too."

I nod. "I feel you."

Rochelle quickly unbuttons her jeans and begins to literally peel them from her legs. As soon as she gets them off of her feet, she tosses them on the floor beside the couch. Now she's lying there in only her wife-beater and panties—and the baseball cap, which, while cool before, isn't quite the image it was when she walked into the room earlier.

"You don't have to keep on the baseball cap," I say. "You can kick back and relax."

She takes it off and tosses it on the floor, too.

I place my hands on her calves and gently massage the backs of her legs, returning slowly to her feet. Her legs are warm, smooth, full, soft. They are the kinds of legs that a man wants to have wrapped around his waist pulling him into the magic that glows between them. I can feel my other head waking up, wanting to force itself into as erect a position as it can in my slacks. I just pray like hell that I can hold it together.

I work my way up to her thigh, patiently moving my thumbs in small circles. She is no longer lying back with her eyes closed. She is looking directly at me, watching every movement of my hands and arms and every expression on my face. I can tell that she knows my breaking point is close, so I try to steer things back across the line into the land of the platonic.

"So where did you grow up?" I ask.

She looks at me, her eyes unmoving. A slight smile escapes her lips. "Newark."

"Newark?" I repeat. "Nice city."

"Yeah," she says, her cat-like eyes looking at me more seductively by the second. "It's a regular Disney World."

Slowly she lifts her other leg toward my hand, and her leg brushes the hardness I have been trying to conceal. She doesn't say anything and pretends to ignore the fact that I could stand up and bang my shit against a wall and leave a hole in the plaster.

"Don't forget this leg," she says, lowering it and resting it back near my crotch.

I feel my erection twitch against her leg, and I suddenly feel like a little boy sitting in a classroom with an uncontrolled hard-on and being asked to walk all the way to the front of the classroom to write an answer on the chalk board for the teacher. She twirls her foot around over the edge of my lap, moving it back and forth slowly. The red toenail polish on each of her toes looks as though she had them done very recently. I trace my gaze from her toes all the way to her black spaghetti string panties. I place my hands on her leg and begin to slowly massage from the foot up.

Suddenly she leans forward, getting my attention. I look to see her unfastening her bra and pulling it out of the shirt opening under her arm. She places it on the floor with the other things.

"Just getting comfortable," she says. "My girls have to breathe."

The only light in the apartment comes from the lamps she turned on when we arrived, but they are more than enough for me to clearly see her nipples piercing the ribbed shirt.

"What are we doing here?" I ask, surprising myself that I can even ask a question this stupid aloud.

"You're giving me a massage," she says. "And a damn good one."

"I see," I say. "You know I'm supposed to write about our date. Are you sure you want to take it any further than this?"

"Cool. I'm just chilling. We ain't done nothing you can't write about."

I grip her leg and pull it toward my erection. She slowly moves her leg back and forth against it.

"This date is supposed to be about compatibility. About seeing if there could be a real connection here," I say, breathlessly.

"You don't feel a connection with me?" she asks, feigning hurt, her leg still stroking me.

My hands move to her thighs, and her legs fall open. I can feel the heat of her sweet spot only inches away from my fingertips.

"We can't do this," I say. "There's too much at stake for us to go at it like this."

She shrugs. "It's a column for a website. There ain't no one else up in here."

She rocks her hips forward and her crotch brushes against my fingers. I can feel the dampness beneath the thin fabric.

"Still," I whisper.

Before I can say anything else, she is unbuckling my pants.

YOU MAY NOW

TURN THIS RECORD OVER

SIDE B

15

Never have I written a piece of fiction grander than I did with that last blog entry for *Soul Sista*. The evening with Rochelle a/k/a Roxanne was one of the most challenging evenings I'd experienced in some time. Even now as I reflect over the movement of her mouth over my body, I wrestle with how I was able to hold out as long as I did. Needless to say, much of what happened I couldn't write in the blog entry. What I ended up writing was more about our musical connection and our quiet dinner and conversation. There was no mention of what happened in Brooklyn or how I cringed at her grammar while still tingling throughout my body from her touch.

In fact, the way the entry reads is that it was the least eventful of my three dates—which is the understatement of the year. But no one seems to notice—or care. Denise runs it without comment, and the only question I get is when will I do my follow-up dates. Just the thought of seeing Sarah again makes me smile, but then so does the thought of seeing Taylor. Still, I feel like I have put too much, too early, into Rochelle and am therefore on the hook with her, at least on some level.

Time to refocus. I have to just settle down and finish what I have started.

❧

As we prepare to close up shop for the evening, J tells me that we need to talk.

"Cool, I want you to take a look at some of the t-shirt designs I had made up."

I walk around to look at his laptop. There are three t-shirt templates on the screen. Team Sarah, Team Taylor, and Team Roxanne. The names are across the chest of each shirt. Beneath the three designs is what I figure will be the back of each shirt: Who will he pick? In slightly smaller print running across the top of the t-shirt is the C&J's Rare Grooves logo, which is our store name written across a vinyl record with a red label.

"So what do you think?" he asks.

As I look at the designs, I start to feel my lips purse tightly. I don't know if it's the stress coming to a head or what, but I feel myself going into a funky space.

"What the hell is this?" I ask. "These are real people, not some characters out of a *Twilight* movie. I don't think this is a good move. At all."

"Man, this is a quick way to milk some sales."

"This is not a reality show! This is real life," I say, unable to control my voice. "Do you think black women are going to sit back and let us make a mockery of the process?"

"Are you fucking kidding me?" J responds,

bouncing back with a voice that he rarely uses with me. "This whole thing is a fucking joke! I mean, think about it. Neither one of us reads that damn magazine, and the only reason any of this is going on is because they finally ran a profile that they'd been sitting on for over four months. Do you think anyone really gives a fuck who you choose? You're probably the only person taking this shit seriously."

"Dude," I start.

"Don't 'dude' me right now, Cool. I sit around here day in and day out while you galavant all over town with these women. This is a partnership, Cool. That means that we both have to put in the work to make this place be what it's supposed to be."

"What do you think I've been trying to do? This is *all* business!" I say.

J shakes his head. "Negro please. These girls got your nose so wide open. It's not about this shop. It's about you trying to hook up with someone."

"You were the one saying that all of this was a good idea. Don't get on me because you're jealous."

"Jealous? I don't have to be jealous about your situation. At least if I have a woman over, I don't have to write about the shit. All I'm saying is that you're falling off and you need to get your priorities in order."

"And what about these t-shirts?" I say, pointing at his laptop, my breathing still heavy.

"Capitalizing on a situation. That's what business people do, Cool."

I stare at him for a moment, my brow furrowed. Then I look back at the t-shirts. Angie's words about me being pimped come to mind again and I feel my blood begin to simmer. "Here I am thinking that I might be getting pimped by the magazine, but it turns out I'm really getting pimped by you."

"You can call it what you want, but in the end, it's all business. I didn't quit my job at J.P. Morgan to be struggling in this cubbyhole. I'm just trying to play the hand I got dealt before all of the chips run out."

"So what are you saying? That we're going to close down?"

He shakes his head as if I am not getting the full picture. "I'm a realist," he says and pauses. "I know that all of this *Soul Sista* stuff'll come to an end and next year we'll be trying to find a new way to stay afloat. Face it, man. We just picked the wrong damn business to get into. If we break even without a loss, we'll have accomplished something."

I shake my head. "We've got to give it time, dude! Rome wasn't built in a day."

"That shit would be cool if we had the right kind of money coming in—which we don't." He stops and exhales, considering his words.

I stare at him, waiting.

He continues. "I'm just stressed, man. Fuck it. I need to get some fresh air. We can pick this shit back up tomorrow."

I swallow hard. "Yeah. Let's do that."

I watch him pack up his computer bag and walk out the front door. For an hour I sit behind the counter staring at all of the things around me: the music from the artists I love, the t-shirts and hats, the posters, and the other merchandise we have packed into our small store.

I remember when we signed the loan papers and all of this became a reality. It wasn't just us sitting around talking about a record store anymore; we were actually doing it. I can also remember when we came up with the name for the store, the logo, and how we would lay the store out. Even before we officially opened, I could feel magic in the air, even while I swept the floors and painted the walls the retro maroon color that they are. I remember thinking how good it felt to stand in my sneakers and jeans in my own place of business, surrounded by the grooves that have served as the soundtrack to my life. Starting this business was like marrying the woman of my dreams.

And she's still the woman of my dreams.

And that is why C&J's Rare Grooves has to survive. There's no question about that. We have invested too much time into this place to just give it up without a fight. I'm hoping cooler heads prevail in the morning.

As I cut off the lights and lock the door, I realize that I will do whatever it takes to keep this place alive—even if that means I have to put on a pair of stilettos and walk my prostituted ass between the damn raindrops.

16

My intention is to call Sarah back first, just to keep things in order, but Taylor beats me to the punch. She tells me about an event over at Central Park and asks me if I'd like to go. Sure, I tell her. At this point it's time to see where we're going with all of this anyway.

I meet her at the Central Park entrance at Columbus Circle, right beside a brilliant golden statue of a woman blowing a horn above a small team of galloping horses. Right through the entrance are trees, lush green grass, and sidewalks branching out into various directions. The temperature is perfect. Taylor couldn't have picked a better day for going to the park. I just have no clue of where she's taking me.

Skyscrapers frame the park, like the elaborate walls of a garden, and the laughter of children and adults mix with the sounds of the traffic moving around us. The smell of a hotdog cart a few feet away beckons me, and my stomach growls, but just as I start to move toward the cart, I remember that

Taylor doesn't eat meat—or cooked things for that matter.

I return my attention to her, trying my best to ignore the scent. Her curly Afro is almost glowing in the sunlight, and her skin looks as if she was fashioned from the same gold as the statue at the entrance. She's wearing a yellow summer dress with red, orange, and brown flowers printed across it. There's also a flower tucked neatly onto the side of her hair. She looks subtle, yet sexy, and I realize that I'm even more drawn to her beauty now than I was when we met the last time.

I reach in to hug her slight frame. "It's good to see you again," I offer, enjoying the snug feel of her body against mine.

"You, too. How have you been?"

"Well, I can't complain. Just trying to put everything together now."

She nods. "I bet you forgot my name until I called you."

I laugh. "I couldn't do that—even if I tried."

"Why's that?"

"You are responsible for the healthiest meal I've ever had in my life."

She laughs in jest.

We walk into the park, and inline skaters and bicyclists move around us. Everyone seems to be enjoying this Saturday morning just as much as we are. But for a minute, I feel a twinge of guilt. While I typically take off two Saturdays a month at the store, I still feel uneasy about my argument with J. Maybe I should have gone in this morning as a good faith gesture to clear the air. But no. I am here with Taylor. I wonder for a moment if J is right about my absences hurting the business. He can't be right. After all, my being on this date is keeping the name of our business in front of several hundred thousand people, free of charge.

"So where're we headed?" I ask.

"To a picnic."

"A picnic? I don't see any food, unless it's tucked in that small bag of yours," I joke, pointing to the tiny hemp purse that hangs from her bare shoulder.

"No. My meditation group is having a picnic. I thought it would be fun for us to drop by."

I don't know why, but this puts me in a weird space. Not that I have anything against meditation —hell, I do it myself from time to time— but it just doesn't feel like the best place for us to be having our date. It's hard enough getting to know someone in an environment where the two of you are alone, but being in a group of people who may not necessarily connect with you is sometimes more trouble than it's worth.

I chuckle uneasily. "Are they all raw vegans, too?"

She laughs. "No. They eat the whole spectrum, so I think you'll be fine."

"So they'll be grilling barbecue over there?"

She shrugs, "Maybe." Then offers, "Probably not."

We continue walking for a quarter of a mile and finally come to a large spot of grass off to the side of the sidewalk.

"Taylor!" a thin redheaded woman calls out from a group of people seated on beach towels. "Over here!"

"Hey!" Taylor answers, taking me by the hand and walking me over to the group.

There are at least ten people of various ethnicities, all dressed casually for the temperature, all of them barefoot. Several weaved baskets sit on the towels and there are paper plates spread around with jars of colorful concoctions, breads, and even cookies on them. She takes me around introducing me to each person. The redheaded woman's name is Phoeba, and she comes across as the leader of the group.

"Cool?" she asks, shaking my hand. "Quite a name you have there."

I nod. "That's what I hear." I look down at the towels. "Nice spread. How long have you guys been out here?"

"Not more than an hour," Phoeba says. She quickly turns to face Taylor. "So this is the guy you met through the magazine?"

Taylor nods, a smile stretched across her face.

"Not bad," Phoeba says. "Not bad."

The moment we sit down with the group, I realize that I will have trouble getting comfortable. Although I work out regularly, my flexibility is still not what it should be, so with no chairs, I find that I'm forced to sit legs-crossed like the others, who clearly have no problems perching themselves like that for extended periods of time. When I grimace trying to position myself, Taylor leans in and says, "You can just lie down on your side. I want you to be comfortable."

So I do. And I'm the only one in the group who's stretched out into the grass like a sick dog, while the others maintain a kind of relaxed and seated balance. I'm also the only one to have on shoes, since I'm leery about being barefoot outdoors —especially in New York City. Immediately, I remember the song from *Sesame Street*: "One of these things is not like the other...."

"Want some potato salad?" Taylor offers, as she reaches for a plate.

"Is it real potato salad or potato-less potato salad?" I ask, half-joking, half-serious.

"Real potato salad," she responds, smiling.

"Sure."

She spoons out some of it and hands it to me with a fork.

As I thank her, I see her look past me and rise to her feet. I angle my head and see a tall, athletic white guy with dusty blond hair. His skin has a hard tan, not one that appears to have been applied at a tanning salon. She immediately runs up to him. As he outstretches his arms and embraces her, they kiss quickly on the lips before she falls completely into his chest. While brief, the entire scene strikes me as far more than platonic. She grabs his hand, as she did mine earlier, and brings him over to me for an introduction.

"Cool? This is Norman. Norman, this is my new friend, Cool."

He extends his hand to me, and I shake it with a firmness typically reserved for old factory guys who get a kick out of trying to roll your knuckles in their hands. He meets me back with a firm handshake, his lips curled into a casual, unflustered smile.

"Mate," he says, nodding to me and releasing my hand.

"I didn't think you were coming," Taylor says, smiling at him as if his last name were Vanderbilt.

"Wouldn't have missed it for the world!" he says, holding back his head and letting out a deep laugh.

Missed it for the world, I think. Really? As far as I can tell, this is just a casual gathering of people on a few feet of grass in an already busy park. Am I missing something here?

I look at Taylor, who leans her back into my chest playfully, still facing Norman. I place my hand on her hip and I feel her fingers brush over my hand. Norman smiles and begins to greet the other people who have risen from their towels. As he steps around us, I lean down and whisper in Taylor's ear, "What was that about?"

"He's just a friend," she responds.

"Oh, okay," I say.

As she turns around to rejoin the group, I take her hand again, pulling her gently toward me. "And what am I?" I ask.

She smiles at me. "Don't be silly," she says. "You're my friend, too."

❧

HOURS LATER, SEATED AT A CAFE ON THE UPPER West Side, we sip tea and watch people walk by. I'm still bothered about earlier, although I can't say specifically why. It's not like we're in a relationship. Still her kissing that guy unnerved me a bit. I try not to think about it too hard. After all, she's had to sit by and read about me going on dates with two other women.

"You all right?" she asks. "Penny for you thoughts."

I look up from my mug and offer a smile. "It's a beautiful day. I'm glad you asked me to come down here."

She nods. "I hope you didn't mind that I shared you with my friends for a few hours."

"Not at all." I am not sure if this is a lie or not.

"So can I ask you a question?"

"Sure."

She interlocks her fingers on the table. "I know this is only our second time going out, but I'm curious. How compatible do you think we are so far?"

I inhale deeply. "I think you're very intelligent, very centered, very focused. You seem like a pretty wonderful woman."

"Mmm," she muses. "You're not really answering my question."

"There's definitely potential," I say.

"Fair enough," she responds.

"So what do you like to do?" Up until that moment it never occurred to me to ask her this very basic question.

"I love yoga! I go at least four times a week, and I am trying to get certified to teach classes."

"Really? I have absolutely no flexibility—as you already know," I say, laughing.

She laughs along with me. "You just have to take it in small steps. I'm pretty flexible, but I am not on the level of some of these people who can bend themselves into the most extreme positions."

"But don't people do a lot of farting in yoga?"

She shakes her head, trying to suppress a smile.

"No more than people would fart doing anything else."

Hearing her say the word "fart" sounds cute coming from her mouth.

"So what is your day job now?" I ask.

"I work at an after school program for at-risk youth. It's pretty cool. I love kids. I hope to have a team of them one day."

"What's a team?"

"At least five."

"Whoa," I say. "You serious?"

"No," she responds, chuckling. "But you should have seen the look on your face. Priceless."

She is so beautiful, and all I want to do is lean across the table and kiss her, but I can't bring myself to follow through. Maybe it's the thought of seeing her kiss that guy from earlier. Even though it wasn't a French kiss, it still looked as if there had been some underlying familiarity in it.

"Taylor? Is that you?" I hear a male voice say from behind me.

"Lewis!" she screams, jumping to her feet. She runs over and wraps her arms around a tall, bearded white guy who, even in the day's heat, gives off the rugged look of a lumberjack on vacation. He leans down and kisses her squarely on the lips in a manner too reminiscent of the kiss I saw from earlier. She brings him to our table and introduces us, and like deja vu, I am looking into the eyes of another man who has apparently had some kind of relationship with her in the past—one that apparently is open enough for her to not be afraid of kissing him around me. I stand and shake hands, put on my best face, and count the minutes until he continues walking down the street.

"I'm just curious," I start, as Taylor and I return to our chairs. "These guys you keep running into, are they ex-boyfriends?"

"I don't do ex-boyfriends."

"What does that mean?"

She sighs. "You remember I told you that I don't believe in titles?"

"So you run simultaneous relationships then?"

"No," she says. I can see she is becoming bothered my implications. "They are all my friends."

I nod. "Well, okay. Let me ask you this: have you ever been intimate with either one of them?"

She shakes her head, clearly annoyed. "Cool, I don't really think that's any of your business. I didn't ask *you* if you were having any intimate relationships with anyone. I mean, for all I know you could have been getting it on with any of these other girls you've been going out with."

I blush, but pray like hell it doesn't show through my brown skin. "I didn't mean to upset you."

"I'm not upset," she responds, "but I think you're assuming a hell of a lot on a second date."

For a moment we sit in silence, and I wonder if it's worth trying to clean up this situation before taking my black ass back to Harlem.

"Can I ask a question?"

"It's a free country," she responds, her voice more curt than I would have expected.

"How often do you go out with black men?"

She smiles, her defenses cracking slightly. "You're the first in a while."

"So why me?"

"Why not you?"

I take her fingers and place a kiss gently atop her hand. She looks at me and smiles.

We continue to sit and talk as the sky darkens around us. When we finally rise to say goodbye, we both realize that we are saying goodbye for more than just the evening.

17

———

I was once at a park in Washington, DC, when I saw a guy riding a bicycle run into a stop sign and get swept clean off of his bike and onto the ground. The funny thing was that the sign had been in front of him the entire time, but he was just so focused on his pedaling that he never looked up to see it. That red octagon was much more than a sign; it was an instruction the man ignored at his own peril. Talk about ironies.

The whole thing had happened so quickly that when he slammed into it, it sounded like the blast of a shotgun. When the crowd of us who had witnessed the accident walked over to him, we immediately knew he was in bad shape. One woman standing there had asked if he was dead. I shook my head. "No, just unconscious," I said. What gave me the license to make that diagnosis? Nothing, other than the fact that I knew for the guy's sake that he needed to be alive so that he didn't find himself the post-humous recipient of the dreaded Darwin Award, one of those recognitions reserved for people who died under the most absurd of circumstances.

Another guy who was standing nearby had already placed a call to 911 for an ambulance. By the time it arrived, the guy was conscious, but dazed. I don't have any idea of how many stitches he had to get to close up that massive gash on his face, but I imagine that he might still be wearing the scar wherever he is in the world today.

I slammed into my metaphorical stop sign when Ray-Ray came in for work on Monday morning. Even now, as I sit here tracing through everything that has happened, I wonder if J and I can rebound from this new turn of events.

I hadn't thought anything initially when Ray-Ray walked in, covering his mouth with his hand and pointing at me.

"Oh snap!" he had said. "Oh snap!"

I looked over at him, confused. "Dude, what's up with you?"

"Tell me you didn't, Cool. Tell me it ain't so!" he said, bending over and stomping around in a small circle like an overexcited preacher.

"Ray-Ray," I said, pulling rank. "Get yourself together. This is a place of business."

He stood up, straightening himself out. "My bad."

"Now," I said, "what's this all about?"

"Word is on the street about you, son! For real!"

"Word about what?"

"You and that vixen. They say you wore her out like Zumba!"

I stood there, my mind racing like Usaine Bolt on juice.

"All I gotta ask," Ray-Ray said, "is was the shit good? A nigga has to know."

At that point everything around me turned into white noise. I could scarcely make out Ray-Ray telling me about the different rappers who had had sex with the infamous Roxanne. All I could think was that the one thing I regretted had come back to haunt me with a vengeance.

By the time J walked in, he was already joining the conversation. "So much for the t-shirt idea," he huffed.

Even Denise had called the store several times, but I couldn't bring myself to call her back. I just needed time to think.

And here I am now. Still thinking. No farther along.

I see J up front googling articles on his computer. He turns back to me. "Cool, these blogs are talking up a storm about you this morning."

I'm not even sure I want to know what they're saying, but J offers me a few comments anyway.

"They say that you were typical, trying to get with the video vixen. But what most people are talking about is how you lied on your last blog entry, talking about it was on some regular date shit. And you know, Roxanne ain't no regular date chick. One guy is even comparing you to Clinton. He's here saying that if you were lucky enough to get some brain, then just be a man about it and own up to it."

"Okay," I finally say. "Enough."

I stand up and stretch my arms. "I'm taking a walk. I need some fresh air," I say, before stepping out of the store into the bright morning sunlight.

ANGIE AGREES TO MEET ME AT A CAFE NEAR Chelsea Piers. While I take a cab down to West 22nd Street, I try to plan my strategy for dealing with everything that's going on. The first thing I want to do is call Rochelle to find out if she knows anything about this stuff. Is this just a rumor coming from neighborhood speculation, or did she actually put the word out herself? I reach for my cell phone and dial her number, but she doesn't pick up. Now I'm left to try to put things together on my own—at least for the time being.

When I pull up to the cafe, I'm relieved to see that Angie is already seated at one of the tables out front.

"Cousin!" she says, standing to embrace me.

"Angie, I can't tell you how good it is to see you right now."

"Baby, calm down and have a seat. You look like you're about to lose it."

I fall into my chair.

"Well, if it's any consolation, I didn't know anything about any of this until you called me, so clearly everybody in New York is not in the know," she chuckles.

I shake my head. "I need to call Denise and find out what the deal is." Then I remember Sarah.

Shit!

This day is getting worse by the minute. If I read her vibe right, she definitely wouldn't touch me with a ten-foot pole if she heard anything about this Rochelle business. Right now I can't think about that though. I have too many other pressing issues.

"Have you talked to that girl yet?" Angie asks.

"I tried to call her from the cab on the way here. I couldn't reach her."

"Cool, with your ties to music and all, I figured you'd recognize that chick from that Big Boze video."

I start chewing my lip, a bad habit I have when my nerves start to work on me. "You know I don't watch music videos on television. My artists don't have a lot of videos in rotation." I shake my head. "So she really was famous then?"

Angie shrugs. "Depends on who you ask. She's famous in a C-list, pin-up girl kind of way."

At times like this, I wish I had gotten more information about these women ahead of time so that I could better vet the situation before going out with them. But what did it say about the readers of *Soul Sista* that they would hook me up on a date with such a notorious woman?

"I'd try her again," Angie says.

I grab my phone and hit redial. This time the phone picks up.

"What, nigga," Rochelle says, her voice flat.

"Rochelle? Is that you?"

"Yeah. What you want?" She sounds as if I am a guy who's calling just to bug her.

"What's wrong with you?" I ask.

"Not a damn thing."

"I heard that people are talking about our date all over town."

"Yeah. So what?"

I pull the phone away from my face and look at it incredulously before speaking again. "Did you do that?"

She laughs in a strange voice and then says, "Fuck you, nigga."

"Whoa," I start, "Talk to me. At least do me that favor. What the hell is going on?"

I hear her sigh. "I just had to set the fucking record straight. You got me looking all green and square in your article. All you had to do is tell the fucking truth, but you couldn't do that. I thought we was connecting. But you just a weak nigga tryna play a sista out."

I squeeze my phone so tightly I fear it might explode in my hands. "I was trying to protect your privacy," I say through gritted teeth.

"Naw, nigga. You was trying to protect yo own ass."

I'm confused by all of this, and I have no words for her. This makes absolutely no sense to me at all. I have no idea of where all of this venom is coming from.

"Okay," I finally say. "I guess I fucked up. I didn't mean to hurt your feelings or anything."

She doesn't respond.

"You still there?"

"Yeah." She's quiet for a moment. Finally, she speaks again. "You know I didn't say nothing except that we had hooked up. You know you can still pick me to be your girl."

You have to be fucking kidding me, I think to myself. This is all about the fucking website?

"At this point, I don't think I could do that even if I wanted," I respond, my jaw so tight I can feel my TMJ starting to bother me.

"A'ight. Whatever," she says, and she hangs up on me.

Angie looks at me, her eyes focused on mine. "Breathe, Cool. Breathe, baby."

I drop my phone onto the table and it sounds like a brick slamming against the hood of a car. "She played me," I say. My head is throbbing, and I just want to go somewhere and lie down.

"That seems like some street shit there. Trying to muscle her way into the spotlight. You gotta just let that shit roll off your back," Angie offers.

My thoughts are bouncing back and forth in my mind like waves slamming against rocks.

"I'm sorry, Angie. I have to go."

She nods and stands up with me. "Hey, it's gonna be all right," she says.

I blink hard and say, "I hope so."

As I start to walk to the curb to hail a cab, Angie follows me. "Hey, Cool. I just wanted to let you know that me and Tracy and Aaron are headed to Birmingham to see Mama this weekend."

I turn around and look at my younger cousin. Her doe-like eyes remind me of when she was that cute little tomboy growing up. She hugs me tightly.

"We're some kind of family, aren't we?"

"You know that," she says.

As she turns to walk away, she smiles at me. I know that she is pulling that smile from the depths of her being, so I give her a smile that she can take with her, too.

18

My one-bedroom apartment is like a cave, dark and cool. That's the way I've always liked it. I even prefer the use of candles to running the lights. Although I have a television, I don't have cable, so most of my energy usage is strictly for my computer and wireless connection, as well as my microwave.

I have gotten to the point where I can walk into my apartment and my eyes adjust to the darkness easily. With only the mild illumination of street-lights creeping through the cracks in the window blinds, I can easily navigate the apartment for hours without actually turning on the lights. My running joke with J is, "I'll be damned if Con Ed makes a sucker out of me!"

Now this cloak of darkness is like a familiar wel-come from the world. Right now it feels like my only refuge. As I grab a soda out of the fridge, I find myself wondering how I'm going to deal with all of this. I still have yet to really clean up what happened with J the other day, and while I know he's my boy and will probably shake off all of that madness as just us being too stressed out and in the heat of the moment, I do want to follow up with him—especially if he's having second thoughts about us keeping our business going. And then there's this mess with Rochelle. My head hurts even when I try to consider the implications of what she's done.

Rather than wait to get put on in a legit way, she had simply decided that she would take matters into her own hands. I call myself having done her a solid by keeping the details of our date low key. I would've never thought that she was the kind of person who was so starved for media attention that she'd tell all of her business (and mine) just to shine the spotlight on herself. Wasn't there a rule out there against kissing and telling or has Karrine Steffens's handbook inspired a new league of women who are hell-bent on changing the game? The raw hustler in me can actually respect what Rochelle did, but the pragmatic businessman in me—the one who has to suffer in behind all of this—does not care for it at all. Right now, I can't even fathom all of the different ways this situation can come back to bite me in the ass.

I know this is not going to go well with Sarah, assuming that she's not living in a bubble somewhere and didn't hear any of this madness. I know I'll still need to follow up with her, just to close things out for the magazine, though. I kind of hope that I can do some Svengali shit that will give me a chance to deal with her on my own merits and not in the defensive mode of responding to Rochelle's comments. I won't hold my breath though.

And then there's the business. If what J said is true about business increasing in behind my doing this *Soul Sista* blog, then not only will readers start to rebel against me, but we'll feel that in our bottom line, too.

I polish off my drink and head into the bedroom to lie down. All I want to do is sleep. If I can just clear my head long enough, I might be able to figure out how to deal with all of this.

❧

I WAKE UP AND MY APARTMENT IS PITCH BLACK. Even beyond the blinds it is dark. I have no clue what time it is, but my stomach grumbles, begging to be fed, so I put on a pair of sneakers and grab my wallet and keys.

It's not until I am standing beneath the street lamp in front of my building, my eyes squinting at the light, that I even check my watch for the time. It's only eight, but in my mind it feels much later. I walk down the street to Ray's Pizza, which is just my shorthand for the actual title: THE Ray's One and Only Original Pizzeria. The irony is that Ray's pizza is far better than the other six Ray's farther down, which all have different owners and origins and slightly different names. I grab two cheese slices and a Coke and cop a squat on one of the stools facing the front window. Outside, people are still milling about in small groups, mostly people from the neighborhood coming and going. Occasionally a group of kids will migrate together on a corner for a few minutes before moving on.

After I finish eating, I pick up my cell phone and call J. When he answers, I can hear Earth, Wind &

Fire in the background, so I know he's still at the store.

"Dude," I start. "I'm sorry. It's just been that type of day."

"I feel you," he responds. "You coming back before we close."

"I hadn't planned on it."

"You okay?" he asks, his voice tinged with concern.

"Dude, I'm just out of it," I respond.

"I tell you what," he says. "Come back to the store, and when we close, we can go and get some drinks somewhere."

My eyeballs are still dry with sleep, but I know I don't want to go back into the cave just yet, so I tell him that I'll meet him in a few minutes.

It only takes about fifteen minutes for me to get there, and when I walk into the store, J is wrapping up his laptop cords to put in his computer bag. Rarely do we have any customers in the store requiring us to keep the shop open past nine, so we tend to lock up like clockwork when closing time comes.

"J," I say, walking over to him. "About the other night. Dude, I don't know what got into me."

"Hey, whatever it was, it got into me, too. I was straight tripping. I guess this shit is a little crazy. It's all like an x-factor. Like no matter how much planning I do, something can just come out of nowhere and play a bigger role than anything else."

I reach out and dap him. "I just wanted to let you know I'm sorry."

"Cool, you didn't even have to say those words.

Baby, we go way back. Some shit you just understand without even having to move your mouth."

"But I really fucked us with this Roxanne thing. She all but killed this blogging gig."

"Think so?" he asks.

"What do you mean?"

"You don't see an up-side to any of this shit?"

I shake my head.

"I suspect even more people are reading your blog entries today than at any other point in time. *Soul Sista* can't be mad at you for driving all of that traffic to their site."

I look away. "They are probably going on there to crucify me for lying about the date."

"Really?" he says. "Have you looked at the site today?"

"No."

J pulls out his laptop and opens it back up. He types in the website information and turns the screen to face me. I scroll through the comments on my blog entry and my jaw almost drops on the floor. While the comments are divided between me being a typical dog, there are other comments defending my fibbing of the last date. One commenter says, "Cool was just being respectful and trying not to paint Roxanne into a corner. The fact that she came back over the top on him has more to do with how classless she is, not him!"

J smiles. "Yeah, Cool. They've been debating you all day, and a lot of people are saying that you did the right thing. Even Michael Baisden put the question to his listeners today on his show. It went something like this: When is it okay to tell a white lie in your relationship? This situation is really putting both you and ol' girl out there."

I continue reading all of the different comments, surprised at the diversity of what's being said.

"And there were some calls for you earlier. A few reporters were trying to get statements, but I told them you weren't here. It's actually a good thing you left, because a lot of people came to the store today hoping to see you and give you their two cents worth. Oh yeah, and Denise Mallory called from the magazine. She's been trying to get at you all day. Man, you need to call her back. At least find out what they're doing on their end."

I hadn't even considered that any of this would happen, and I'm still having trouble digesting it all.

When nine o'clock comes, we lock up the shop and J makes good on his promise to get me drunk.

19

I stumble into the store earlier than usual and take care of inventory while trying to shake the remnants of my micro-hangover. By the time J comes in, I am already in full productivity mode. He smiles and starts making calls to follow up with our vendors. Ray-Ray comes in and surprisingly starts dusting the shelves. I suspect he feels bad about yesterday, but he doesn't say anything. Neither do I.

When I finally call Denise Mallory back, I am immediately patched through.

"Hi," she answers. "My, you've been busy."

"You have no idea."

She doesn't waste time and cuts right to the chase. "Do you have plans for lunch?"

I shake my head before realizing that she can't see my face. "Uh, no. I don't."

"Can you meet me at Blockheads on 33rd and 3rd at around 12:30?"

"Sure. That shouldn't be a problem."

When I hang up the phone, J immediately asks what she wanted. Apparently he has invested himself in the process to the point that he wants the blow-by-blow whenever there is any update.

"She wants to talk over lunch in about an hour down in Murray Hill."

"For real? That's crazy. No telling what they're coming up with down there. They could be putting together something even bigger than this blogging thing." He pauses and considers all of this. "What if they are looking to pitch a TV show idea or something? That would be straight crazy!"

I laugh under my breath. "That doesn't make a lot sense, but I'll walk in there with an open mind and hear out anything that they throw at me that could help us out here."

"That's what's up, Cool." J looks at the Michael Jackson clock on the wall. "You might want to get your ass moving, though. You got a little ways to go if you're trying to make it there on time. Don't want to keep Denise waiting. If she lays out a plan that can take this shit to the next level, she'll be my new favorite person—and you can tell her I said that shit."

I laugh. "Don't tempt me, dude. You know I will."

I start walking toward the door, but I stop and turn toward Ray-Ray. "So what's my popularity rating today?" I ask, my smile undermining my attempt at a serious tone.

Ray-Ray laughs, relieved. "Son, I think you might be up in the polls. Folks wasn't feeling that Bohemian chick you hollered at, but the niggas is really feeling this Roxanne thing."

"What about Sarah?" I ask, just to see what he will say.

"She a'ight, but word is that you done already won the jackpot."

I consider this as I walk out of the store and down the sidewalk to catch the bus. I guess I should, at the minimum, be thankful that Roxanne didn't dog me while she was telling our personal business.

Still the whole situation feels a little foul. I'm game to make lemonade from all of this, but I still recognize what the deal is and what kind of game she's running. Clearly she won't be the pick, and now that I think about it, she probably never had plans to be the one anyway.

&

DENISE IS ALREADY SEATED IN THE RESTAURANT checking her Blackberry when I walk through the front door. She looks up and smiles, and I remember just how much I enjoy seeing that smile.

She stands. "How many of those things do you have?" she jokes, pointing to my C&J Rare Grooves t-shirt.

"You don't want to know," I respond, shaking her hand.

"Well, no one can ever accuse you of failing to market your business." She chuckles and returns to her seat.

"Why should Russell Simmons have all of the fun? I mean that brother hasn't been seen wearing anything other than Phat Farm since the mid-nineties."

"True."

"I'll get you one of these—in any color—but you'll have to promise to wear it."

"I see," Denise says, smiling. "If you send me one, I will definitely wear it."

"Outside, I mean. You have to do more than just sleep in it. I have a cousin who uses hers to cut grass in."

She laughs and promises me that she won't use the t-shirt as a dust cloth either.

I sit down perpendicular to her, still unsure if this is an "Everything's going well, glad to see you" meeting or if this is a Bill Duke/*Menace II Society* "you know you fucked up" kind of meeting. She seems in good spirits, so I'll suspend judgment until she gives me a reason to get on high alert.

"You ever eat here before?" she asks.

"Not since I first moved here. These burritos are big as hell though."

"Definitely not for the feint of heart," she offers, smiling.

A server appears at our table and proceeds to take our order. We both order the giant world famous Blockheads burritos and sodas.

When the server walks away, I say, "Watch out now. Eating a meal that big will have you falling asleep all over your desk this afternoon. Just wait until that 'itis' creeps up on you."

"I really don't even need to be eating any of this. I'll have to work out extra time at the gym just to take it all off."

"Are you kidding?" I ask. "You look like you could run a marathon this Saturday if you wanted."

"Ha ha," she says, each syllable pitched in sarcasm.

"Ha ha hell," I respond, laughing. "You know you look good."

"Yeah. Whatever." She offers a smile, before taking a sip of the soda the server has just placed down in front of her.

I take a sip of my own drink and suddenly think back to Sinbad's comedy routine when he says it is impossible for a man to look macho while pursing his lips and sipping from a straw. To hell with it. I take another long swallow, not caring if I look like a brown Fraggle with a doozer stick in his mouth.

"So," she starts. "Cool, please tell me what's going on here."

"What do you mean?" I say.

I know it's really too late to play dumb, but I'm not jumping out there blind. I don't know what she knows, and I would rather take my cue from her rather than incriminate myself for no reason.

"Did the date with Roxanne really happen the way you say it did?" she asks.

I pause for a moment and consider this. Her phrasing of the statement is probably the most diplomatic way that she can muster for asking me if I straight-up lied on my blog entry. My mind races with how I want to answer her question. I guess that's the problem when you start shifting the truth: you find yourself continually having to shift it.

As I take in Denise's solemn facial expression, I decide that I should be honest with her. After all, she doesn't seem like she has a desire to burn me at the stake and sacrifice my ashes to the townspeople.

"I might've taken a few creative liberties," I say. "But it was because I was trying to be respectful."

Denise's expression doesn't change. It's as if she already knows everything that I'm going to tell her before I open my mouth. When she finally speaks, she asks, "So you did have sex with her?"

I start to wonder how any of this came to matter, but then my mind goes directly to Rochelle and I realize that the moment she made her statement to whomever it was, she gave everyone permission to ask whatever they wanted to know about that third date.

"I'm a grown man, and she's a grown woman, and frankly that's all I'm going to say about that."

Denise nods. "Personally, I couldn't care either way, but it's my job to get to the bottom of all of this. So from what you're telling me, you're not going to deny the fact that Roxanne was telling the truth. Well, that just means you'll have to write a retraction on your last entry, and we'll have to see if we can go ahead wrap all of this up."

"A retraction?" I respond. "You want me validate her story to the world? I'm not going to do that."

"Validate her story?" Denise says. "Apparently her story is the truth and yours is just some fluff you threw together to fool our readers."

My breathing quickens. "I'm not the bad guy here. Isn't there anything to say about privacy? I mean, I may as well take the readers into the bathroom with me while I'm at it."

Denise begins to shake her head. "Cool, you're missing the point here. *Soul Sista* is not concerned with your sex life or anything that intrudes on your personal space. Our bottom line is that you lied. Now our credibility is on the line. If we have one columnist spinning fictions, then where does that leave us with how readers perceive the rest of our content?"

"Come on," I say exasperated. "Even people on the forums agree with me."

"Yeah, I heard about the Michael Baisden Show. And while that is all fine and good, Rachel, the editor-in-chief, is taking the position that we need to cover our asses in behind all of this."

"And leave my ass out in the wind in the process," I say.

The server reappears with our orders, but now my appetite is beginning to wane.

"You know," I continue, "I can't write a retraction. I'm not going to give everyone the pleasure of knowing my confidential business. I understand where you guys are coming from—and I respect your positions—but I have to be true to myself on this one."

Denise places her fork down on the table. "My boss is not going to like that. She's likely to scrap the column and issue a statement on your behalf anyway."

I push my plate away from me. I'm no longer hungry, and I'm clueless as to why we are doing all of this over lunch, Jerry Maguire-style. I look her dead in her eyes and say, "Do you really hate me that much?"

She stares back at me incredulously. "Don't be so self-righteous, Cool. This is all business."

I signal the server for my ticket.

"Business?" I respond, as the server hands me the ticket for the table. I pay for both of our meals and stand up.

"Sir, would you like a doggy bag?" the server asks me.

My pride won't let me say yes.

As the server walks away thanking me for the tip, I look down at Denise.

"You're right. This is all business. So you'll have to excuse me while I get back to taking care of mine."

She doesn't say anything as I leave her at the table with two giant burritos and an empty chair.

20

If it weren't for the step team, J and I would probably have never become friends. He was a lanky brother from Chicago, and I was a very average guy from a small place in Mississippi that few people had ever heard of, that is unless they were Civil War buffs. The step team was probably the only way you would find the mix-match pair of us interacting in any meaningful way.

We were both stepping for our freshman step team and were glad to be in the last nine guys standing after tryouts for the team ended. We both stayed in Hubert Hall, but on different floors. Back then, each floor had its own swagger, so my floor was considered the Book Worm floor, while J's floor was considered Playa Central. Ironically, his floor produced the valedictorian for our graduating class, and a guy from my floor went on to become a porn star in Van Nuys, California.

J was one of the few people on our team who'd actually been a part of a step team before coming to college, so he was an obvious choice for the team when the upperclassmen held tryouts. I, on the other hand, was not the most obvious pick for reasons I would only discover after I joined the team.

Yes, I had a sense of rhythm, largely the by-product of my younger days as the resident Michael Jackson impersonator for my family, but it takes much more than a sense of rhythm to be a stepper. It takes conditioning, balance, precision, energy, enthusiasm, a level commitment rarely used outside of organized team sports, and a beast-like rawness that must be summoned upon command at the drop of a dime—even if your lungs are burning so hard from exhaustion that you think they will explode into a million tiny pieces of pink pulp.

But the main reason I wasn't as obvious a choice is because I was too regular. At 5'10 and 150 pounds, there wasn't a lot about me that would stand out on a stage with eight other guys. As I would later learn, the most dynamic-looking steppers tended to be the really hefty brothers or the really small brothers—or, on occasion, that one tall, skinny dude (like J) who was always sticking out his tongue and giving the girls the "I will lick you cross-eyed" look. The thing about the heftier brothers is that no one expects them to be able to keep up with the rest of the group—not on an intense show—so often times the big guy will just stand onstage looking out of place. But this is a ruse, because as soon as the step show comes to his part, he will set it out like nobody's business and bring down the house. In the years since I stepped, both Greek and non-Greek, I've seen this technique used repeatedly, always successfully. The same thing goes for the smaller brother, who can often be overlooked on the stage and sometimes thought of as too slight to make much of an impact. But time and time again I have seen smaller brothers step harder and with more energy than everyone else. When this happens, people tend to go ape shit. One time I even saw a smaller brother step so hard that be actually broke one of the boards on the stage.

But I was neither big nor small—nor even lanky. I was just one of the standard looking steppers who helped those other guys to stand out even more. But to my credit, there were more of us than of them—as it should be. Clearly, everyone can't be Michael Jordan.

Our team didn't win the big show that year, but J and I became best friends. It turns out that we were both business majors, too, although neither of us had taken a course in our major yet. We also did a lot of our female scoping together, moving back and forth between Clark Atlanta and Spelman with comfort and ease. We were wingmen for the other and when we finished freshman year, we got an apartment together in Smyrna. We both kept a rotating door for women we dated, but when I met Rhonda all of that changed.

J didn't trust her off the bat, and that bothered me. I was so into her that when he told me that I shouldn't take myself off the market for her (in essence, that I could do much better), I stopped speaking to him for two weeks. I even considered moving out of the apartment altogether. The only thing that stopped me was the fact that I didn't have enough money to cover all of the rent for a new apartment by myself.

I stayed, but I told him that Rhonda was my girl, and he would just have to respect it. After that, he never made a bad comment about her again. Even when Rhonda and I broke up and he had every single opportunity to gloat and rub it my face, he didn't say a word. He just asked me if I was going to be okay and offered to take me to Little Nikki's Strip Club to help me get over my pain and anguish.

That's when I knew we would be friends for life.

I'll never forget the advice he gave me that night. "Relationships are like B-sides and remixes," he had said.

I laughed. "Is that some kind of Forrest Gump-type wisdom?"

"Not even," he responded. "If women were like records, you'd only see the A-side—the side they wanted you to see. But if you stuck around long enough, you might see the B-Side and the changes that go along with having both sides out there."

I nodded my head, but I didn't know what the hell he was talking about at the time, nor did I care. I was still feeling the pain in my chest from Rhonda's stilettos marching up and down my body. As I started dating on the rebound, what J said started to make more sense. After a few weeks of going out with a woman, the B-Side would come out and put an end to the fun and the newness of it all. But rather than hope I'd find a woman with a nice B-Side, I just felt content to stay on the A-Side. If shit got too heavy, I'd just change records. Plus, I needed to focus on getting other aspects of my life together, things like my cash flow.

At that time I didn't know that J and I would both end up with jobs on Wall Street or that we would ever open a business together in Harlem. Growing up in Mississippi, my plans for the future had been far more conservative than that, and I don't think I would have ventured to dream that big if J hadn't had my back the whole time.

Now as I consider how fucked up the situation will become with *Soul Sista*, I wonder if it's really possible that I may have single-handedly sunk our fledgling business.

It makes me think about Bill Clinton's impeachment. They can say it was all about his lying under oath, but we all know that the reason Congress came down on him like a trapeze artist who missed the bar was because he got his dick sucked AND got caught. And while I wasn't under oath, the editors at the magazine have clearly decided that they have absolutely no interest in standing by me. I guess I can't totally blame them, but I would think that all of these people discussing me could be something that they could play up in a positive and productive way and not just an "it stinks so run from it as fast as we can" kind of way.

I know that J is going to stand behind me on this, but I hate that I even have to put him through any of this. He definitely didn't sign on for it. Neither did I, for that matter.

Still, I just can't roll over and play dead on my dream.

I don't know exactly how I can make things right, but I know that I don't plan on sitting on my ass and allowing my fate to be determined by other people. That was never part of the plan, and I refuse to start incorporating any of that nonsense right now.

21

There's a message on the table in the back of the store telling me that Rhonda called, and while I'm curious to find out what she wants, I know I need to talk to J and Ray-Ray first.

I call an emergency meeting and put a "Will Return in an Hour" sign on the front door before locking it.

As the three of us head to the back of the shop and gather around the small folding table that functions as our de facto conference room, I tell them about what happened at my lunch meeting with Denise and how I think there'll be some fallout in behind my Roxanne journal entry.

"Why don't you just do the retraction? You could just say that you were trying to be respectful of Roxanne and everything. You two were clearly consenting adults, and with that comes a code of discretion. I doubt if anyone would hang you out to dry on something that basic," J offers.

I nod, wanting to believe him. "What do you think, Ray-Ray?"

Normally, Ray-Ray wouldn't be a part of these

meetings, but because of his knowledge of what the word on the streets is, I can't avoid leaving him out of the loop now. I can tell that he's happier than a kid in a candy store, too. This is probably the moment he's been waiting for since we hired him nearly eight months ago.

He leans in as if he's one of the delegated captains of a crime family. "I don't know, Cool. Most everyone thinks you blew your chance with that dancing chick. And I think that you would be crazy retarded to think of riding anything out with that ol' girl Roxanne. You know how many dudes done run up through there. At least you can say that you done hit something that's been beat out the frame by some famous niggas."

"Damn," J says.

I quickly interject. "Ray-Ray, I'm talking about the magazine. What are your thoughts about the magazine?"

I'm still a little thrown off by his comment, but I'm desperate to refocus all of our collective attention to the problem at hand, which in my mind is *Soul Sista*, not Rochelle. But maybe I'm fooling myself. I look at Ray-Ray, hoping the next thing he says is more relevant than the last.

"It's just one mag. It's not like you're being blacklisted across the industry. If you don't feel like you owe a motherfucking cripple crab a crutch, then I would shoot them the deuces. I'd be like 'Peace!' I'm just saying. You could blog your own shit by this point. Folks that care will find you. Those that don't care, well you know."

Up until this moment I've never even considered

the prospect of taking control of my own story outside of the *Soul Sista* website.

"What do you think about me doing my own site, J?" I ask.

He lifts one eyebrow as he mulls this over.

"What are you thinking, dude?" I ask.

"I'm thinking that Ray-Ray might be on to something, but there're a number of other factors you might want to consider."

"Like what?"

"This thing could easily blow over in a week or two, and people would forget that any of this even happened or that it was you who was involved in any of this," J says. "Then the flipside is if you actually keep the blog going, putting all of your business out in the streets like that, at what point would you actually stop? Would you just keep going until you met a woman and decided to get married?"

Hearing J say that aloud makes me realize just how absurd some of the implications are. I keep reminding myself of what Angie said: They are pimping you. Would I not be pimping myself at this point though?

I shrug. At this point I just don't know anything anymore, but one thing becomes clear: I will have to let some of this marinate on my brain before I commit to a course of action. Maybe if I sit still long enough, the best course of action will come into view.

I thank both J and Ray-Ray for their suggestions, and we wrap up the meeting. As we change the sign on the front door and reopen the store, I'm surprised to see a familiar face standing next to the door.

As soon as our eyes meet, I know that things are not about to get better any time soon.

❧

IT'S BEEN NEARLY TWO WEEKS SINCE I SAW HER, and she's easily just as dazzling as she was the moment I first laid eyes on her. This time, however, she's not wearing a black mini-dress. She's dressed in form-fitting jeans and a baby tee that says Harlem Diva.

"Sarah," I say.

"Cool," she responds. "Got a minute?"

There's a little boy inside of me that wants to just break ship and run, but the rest of me needs a sense of closure, if that's what it's going to be. After all, this beautiful woman has been waiting a long time to hear from me, and she's done everything that anyone has ever asked her to do with regard to this situation.

We step out of the store and start down the sidewalk.

"How have you been?" I start.

"It's been going," she offers.

I nod, unsure if she wants me to take the lid off of things first or if she wants to unleash her thoughts, minus my interference.

We walk for another half a block not really speaking, so I start. "What are your thoughts?"

She looks at me out the corners of her eyes. "You mean about us or about you and that other girl?"

"Both," I say.

"Well, what you did with someone else doesn't

really concern me. But if you were looking to add me as another notch to your belt, then you're sorely mistaken."

"I wasn't even thinking that," I say.

She stops cold and turns to face me. "Cool, you really made a fool out of me, didn't you? Here I am thinking that you were this really nice guy, the kind of guy that a sista could grow with, maybe build something with, but you turned out to be just like every other guy. And while that really shouldn't mean a lot to me, my friends and family were following your blog, waiting to see how things would go with us, and then you dog me like this."

"I didn't dog you like anything. We had a great evening together before all of this mess happened. I didn't plan any of this stuff. I was just going with the flow."

"You were just being a ho," she says.

I laugh. "So I'm a ho because I had a one night stand?"

"Yes."

"Yes? Miss 'I would rock your world if you didn't have to write about it'?"

"That's not fair," she says. "I was flirting."

"Yeah, maybe. But I didn't judge you because of it." I rub my fingers across my temples. "You know, Sarah, I really think you're a beautiful woman with a wonderful personality. You're definitely the kind of woman I would've asked out—even if this *Soul Sista* thing never happened—and I can understand why you're upset. I can't even blame you, if I am being real here. I wish there was something that I could say to change everything that's happened, to roll back the clock, to give us a chance to see what could really happen with this situation if we didn't have all of these outside factors at work."

She looks at me, her face solemn and unchanged.

"Does that sound like something that you would like to try?" I ask, looking into her eyes, hoping to capture any connection that we might have had at any point prior to the Rochelle situation.

She shakes her head weakly. "You know I can't do that."

"You can't or you won't?"

She shakes her head. "No matter what would happen between us, this would always be the beginning of our relationship, this funky situation, and I can't have that. I don't think it would be good for either of us."

I sigh. "So this is it, then?"

"It has to be," she says.

"Well," I offer, "I'm sorry to have even put you through this."

"Yeah," she responds. "But I'm a strong woman. Trust. I'll be quite all right."

I lean in to hug her goodbye, but she steps back from me. I nod.

"Maybe in another life," I offer.

"Maybe," she responds, as she walks away.

I stare at the phone for a good five minutes before picking it up and calling Rhonda back. She answers on the third ring, right before I prepare to hang up.

"Hello," she says, and I immediately remember the first time I ever called her, just a few hours after our meeting at the bookstore. I remember thinking about how melodious her voice sounded—as if she could say any simple sentence and it would become music once it passed through her lips. Her voice was light and soft, very sweet and sensual. I could really appreciate her voice because I had dated women in the past who had lower, heavier voices, women, who if they were to smoke, were not far from sounding like Weezie from *The Jeffersons*.

"Hey," I respond. "This is Cool."

"I know," she says. I can tell she is smiling by the lilt in her voice. "It's good to hear your voice," she adds.

"It is good to hear yours, too," I say reluctantly.

"I saw you in *Soul Sista*, and I've been following

your blog. Sounds like you're living a pretty exciting life."

"I guess that's one way to put it," I say. I lie back on my bed, staring into the blackness of my bedroom, imagining the ceiling somewhere in the distance above my head. "How have you been?" I ask. I am not so much curious as I am trying to be polite.

"I am well, and Treasure is well, too."

"I saw her picture on Facebook. She looks just like you."

"That's what people tell me," Rhonda says. "I guess I'm the only one who sees any traces of Craig in her."

My jaw tenses when she says his name. Although I have never seen his face, my imagination has constructed a million combinations for a football player-looking brother. In some of my versions he is a dark brother, like Wesley Snipes, a guy with a smooth baritone voice and muscles like he's been pumping iron since birth. In other versions he's a tall Christopher Williams-looking brother with some heft to go along with that curly hair. I could've easily walked past this dude a million times and not even known it, which made me feel all the more like the world's biggest fool. In all of the versions, though, I hated this nigga's guts with Hatfield-McCoy-type passion. Now I finally have a name, but I don't have the curiosity for much more than that.

"Are you still in Atlanta?" I ask, hoping to push the conversation forward.

"Newport News, Virginia. I've been at NASA for about six years now."

"Nice. And you're not married?"

"Not anymore. Things didn't work out with Craig."

I start to say, "Serves you right," but there's no need to. At this point I'm supposed to play the role of the magnanimous ex-boyfriend, and I plan to do just that. Instead I say, "I'm sorry to hear that. But things are going well now, I take it."

"It can always be better; it can always be worse," Rhonda says. " Look, Cool. I know that I'm probably the last person in the world that you expected to hear from, and I'm probably the last person in the world you actually care to hear from. I was just thumbing through the magazine and saw your picture, and it made me realize some things."

"Like what?"

"Like the fact that I really hurt you. I really did you wrong."

"It took a picture of me in a magazine for you to realize that?"

She sighs. "Life has just been moving so fast, and I haven't had a lot of time to fret over things in my past. It's hard raising a little girl alone. So yes, it took me seeing your picture to really grasp the other side of what went down between us."

I can feel that old anger beginning to bubble beneath the surface, but I push to hold it at bay. "So you did me wrong. That was a long time ago."

"Well, maybe. But I know that sometimes we change ourselves to deal with the situations that affect us the most. I open a magazine and see you're an eligible bachelor, and I know deep down in my heart that you're a great guy who could easily have any woman he wanted. I can't help thinking that the reason you don't is because you don't trust women the way you used to."

I scoff. "Aren't YOU the dime store psychologist?"

"I'm just telling you what I think, but that's not why I reached out to you," Rhonda says.

I lower my forehead into my hand. "So why did you reach out to me then?"

She hesitates, and I have a fleeting thought that maybe she lied about Craig being Treasure's father. I brace myself for anything.

"Cool," she starts, "I just wanted to tell you that I was sorry. Sorry about everything: the way I did you, the way I hurt you."

I start laughing softly at first, as if she is telling me some kind of joke.

She says it again. And again.

Slowly I feel my throat stiffen, and I can only sit there with the phone cradled next to my face. I'll be damned if I sit up here and unleash nine years of pain in a huge ball of snot and tears for her edification. Instead I want to just be left alone to understand the sense of relief that comes with knowing that I was not crazy for what happened, that I had not romanticized the past unnecessarily, that I was a good man to her.

"I know this is all too little too late," she adds, "but I wanted you to hear those words directly from me. None of what happened with us was your fault. You had never done anything to me to deserve what I did. There were just a lot of things beyond your control."

I am silent as I listen to her.

"Not that you asked, but my relationship with

Craig had never officially ended after my father died during my freshman year. He had been there for me, and when he left for the summer and started dating another girl, I was hurt. Then you came along, and you were wonderful and I really liked you."

"But you never loved me," I say.

She pauses before answering, "Not the way you wanted me to."

I see myself as a senior in college with dreams of spending my life with her. I had absolutely no clue that I was alone in my thinking, and that thought makes me feel foolish now—nine years later.

"So what now?" I ask. "Are we supposed to be friends?"

"I don't know, Cool. I guess all of that is up to you. I just wanted to let you know that I felt bad for the way things turned out. If you never want to speak to me again, I can totally understand that— and respect that."

I massage my temples with my fingers. "Well, I appreciate your telling me everything. You know what's fucked up though? The illusion of shared history."

"What do you mean?" she asks.

"When two people experience something, and one of those people thinks the world of it, but the other doesn't. That's the illusion of shared history. That's me walking around looking at our memories with this perfect golden lining around them and you looking at them as expendable things that you just lived through."

"I wouldn't put it like that," she says.

"Well, how would you put it then?"

She says, "What we experienced was great. It's just that we were at two different emotional places at the time."

As I consider this, I realize that I have to let all of this weight go. I have carried it with me for so long that I thought it was a part of me. I can't change anything that has happened in the past, to me or to her, but I can change how I choose to be in this moment.

"Thank you," I say.

"For what?" she says.

"For giving me the opportunity to deal with the truth directly."

She is quiet for a moment.

"Maybe one day we could be friends again," she says.

I lift my head and look out into the darkness of my room, my eyes now better adjusted.

"Maybe," I say, but at this moment I cannot tell if I am telling the truth or not. I can only tell that I need time, the kind of time that sheds the past to make space for the future.

23

While my life has been going in what feels like a million different directions at once, J has been implementing his earlier plan of getting an open mic poetry event going. The three of us have since been throwing ourselves into this idea whole-heartedly. After some brainstorming, we figured out a way to accommodate a small crowd of people and still maintain floor space for our products. J expects roughly fifty or so people to show up. I expect more —more than what I feel we can comfortably accommodate, but I want to see his idea succeed, and I figure having too many people want in is the kind of problem that we'd actually want to have, versus the alternative.

Sitting around allowing our marketing to be anchored by *Soul Sista* has run its course. We didn't ask anyone's permission to exist, and it makes little sense that we would stop trying to push ourselves to the next level on our own blood, sweat, and tears. At the end of the day, if we allow the situation at *Soul Sista* to sink us, then that's on us. We can't spend our days feeling like we have little control over what we've created.

As we review our checklist for the event, the store phone rings.

"Hello?" I answer.

"May I speak to Cool Brown?"

I can tell by the sweetness of her voice that it is Denise, and I want to kick myself for even thinking about the sound of her voice in that way.

"This is he. Denise, is that you?"

She laughs. "Yes. You're good," she says.

"I just know your voice. That's all," I respond.

"I wanted to call you first."

I shake my head, but I know she can't see me. "You just wanted to let me know that the final nails have been placed in my coffin?"

She chuckles. "I guess I should apologize for the way things went down the last time we met up. I had a lot if time to think about what you said. So I went back to my boss and told her that we should stand behind your decision to not do the retraction."

All of this is new to me, so I sit quietly, listening to make sure that she is saying what I think she is.

"I convinced her to let you finish what you started, and the editors will issue a statement acknowledging a respect for your privacy as you make your selection."

Now I feel like an ass. I can still remember the way I walked out on her, leaving her with those two gigantic Blockheads burritos. I immediately launch into my own apology.

"I never should have walked out on you like I did. I'm sorry I did that."

"Don't sweat it," she says. "I know the situation was tight, so I can't blame you. No telling how I would've felt if it had been me in the same situation."

"So where do we go from here?" I ask.

"You just pick up where you left off and do the best you can to finish your dates and make a decision," Denise says.

"They're all gone."

"Who? All of the women?"

"Yes," I say.

"So you're telling me that none of the three situations has any potential left in them?" Denise asks, her voice beginning to turn.

"Nada."

"Oh shit," she mutters in a way that concerns me.

"What? Talk to me," I say.

"It's just that I fought for you to get this chance. Now I feel like a damn fool."

My mind begins to race with different ideas. I definitely don't want her to catch flack from something she was doing for me as a favor.

"Don't worry. We can figure out something," I say, not having a clue as to what I'm talking about. "Do you want to grab a drink after work or something? We can come up with something."

I can tell she's pondering this. When she finally opens her mouth to speak, she tells me to meet her at the BBQ's down in the Village, the same location of my date with Taylor that went awry. I agree, hoping to put her at ease while I discuss a few options with J and Ray-Ray.

It's already 3:00 in the afternoon, roughly three hours before I'm supposed to meet up with her, and while that might seem like a long time, when you don't have a clue as to how to fix a situation that seems largely beyond your control, that three hours may as well be five minutes.

&

AFTER TALKING WITH J AND RAY-RAY, I'M NO closer to a solution for this latest development. J wants me to revisit Taylor for the sake of bringing about a conclusion that at least makes sense on a fundamental level. Ray-Ray suggests that I just argue for three new girls, citing Flavor Flav's second season of *Flavor of Love* as an example. I decide that there is another option that no one has thought of yet, and as I find my way to BBQ's, I have no clue whatsoever of what that other option is.

I actually arrive before Denise does, so I stand outside under the awning waiting and watching people walk by. Standing there feels like deja vu. I half-expect to see Taylor with her curly, fluffy brown Afro walking by. I can still remember the glow of her golden skin and how I had once wanted to be wrapped in her arms and legs. Then I see her with her "friends," the men she can't bring herself to call "ex-boyfriends," and I'm reminded that I would've never been able to have a committed relationship with her. Personally, I just don't think she really wanted one. Another side of me wonders if I could've been in a relationship with a woman who didn't eat anything that I did. On the surface it's easy to say that something like that is not a big deal, but after a barbecue or two, I don't know if I would still feel the same way. I could never cook my favorite dishes for her or share my favorite restaurant meals with her. I know it sounds trivial, but food can be sexy to me, and I feel like that would be something we would have missed out on.

Almost completely lost in my thoughts of Taylor, I almost don't notice Denise easing up on me.

"Hey, Cool," she says, her voice tired and not as buoyant as it was earlier.

"Denise," I say, taking in her tired look. "Please give me a smile, or I'll feel like I have destroyed your week."

She musters a smile, just enough for her dimples to appear.

"We're gonna kill some fried wings and a few drinks and come up with something so that everybody is happy."

Denise shrugs and follows me inside. We are seated near the back of the restaurant.

"I just don't know how we can fix any of this. You will have to tell me what happened with these women where you ended up empty-handed."

I start with my last date with Taylor and explain to her why things didn't work out. Then I explain the Rochelle situation and how it adversely affected my connection with Sarah.

"How do you fix any of that?" Denise asks.

I shrug my shoulders. "I haven't quite figured that part out yet. Is it possible to get some more selections from your readers?"

Denise shakes her head. "Rachel already didn't want to spend any more time and effort on this, so I seriously doubt she would give you any more chances. Whatever you choose to do has to be done with the situation you've already started."

"Something told me you were going to say that," I respond. "Well, what if I just write one last entry saying that I couldn't find someone from the three women the readers selected?"

Just then, the server appears and takes our orders. We settle on piña coladas with 151 shots and a giant plate of fried wings.

"I thought about that, too. It would be the truth, but it would be awfully anti-climactic."

I nod. "But it would be the truth, and that has to count for something, especially since I've already been accused of being dishonest."

Denise smiles. "This whole thing is just proving to be much more than I had anticipated."

"This was your idea?"

She laughs. "I thought you knew that."

"Well, now I do. I'm curious. Why me and not some other Joe?" I ask.

"You were the one who got the most mail, and from reviewing your bio, you just seemed like a pretty decent guy, someone who could do this thing in such a way that it would be both entertaining and classy."

I nod. "You know, my cousin told me that I shouldn't have ever done this, that I was pimping myself by doing all of this."

"That was never my intention," Denise says.

I shrug. "Either way, I have to say that this proves to be much more than I think either of us expected."

The server appears and places our Texas-sized drinks on the table. We lift the 151 shots.

"A toast to making sense of all of this," I propose.

"Sounds good to me."

As our plastic tubes clink, I decide to relax and let all of the cards fall where they may.

24

After three drinks Denise and I are no closer to a resolution, but we have managed to compare notes on every important R&B album of the 80s and 90s.

"*NE Heartbreak* was a great album, but Bobby Brown's *Don't Be Cruel* was a more important album for his career," Denise says.

I laugh. "You're basically comparing the production of Jimmy Jam and Terry Lewis to the production of Teddy Riley. That's like comparing apples and oranges."

"Maybe. But Teddy owned that period in music. Keep in mind Keith Sweat's first album had just dropped and Guy's first album was on the way."

I smile. Denise and I must have been born from the same pod. "Not to be too hyperbolic here, but New Jack Swing saved my life!"

"Yours?" she says, grabbing the last wing on the plate. "I can't tell you how many times I played that New Jack Swing remix to that Jane Childs song!"

"I Don't Wanna Fall in Love," we both say at the same time and burst into laughter.

I look at the fact that our glasses are empty and the plate has only crumbs and bones from the fried wings.

"Want me to order us some more drinks—and wings?" I ask.

"You know what I really want?" she says.

"No," I say chuckling. I can still feel the buzz of the alcohol flowing through my body.

"I really want some Hershey Kisses!" She giggles like a schoolgirl, and I can tell that we are both a little tipsy.

"Will a kiss from a chocolate brotha do?" I ask. I have no earthly idea what made me say that, but it feels as natural as anything else in my current state of relaxation.

"I don't know," she responds. "Let me see." She leans forward and kisses me quickly on the lips before sitting back and saying, "Nah, I need a real Hershey's Kiss."

"Damn, it's like that?" I laugh, still dazed that she kissed me. It all happened so quickly that my lips didn't even register it. I'm guessing we will need to stop the alcohol for the evening. It would be too crazy if we did something even more reckless, something that we both might regret later.

"Your lips are nice, but they're not chocolate."

"So where can we pick up your candy?" I ask.

"At the Hershey Store in Times Square!"

I laugh. "We have to pass at least a hundred stores that sell Hershey's Kisses before we even get to Times Square, though."

Denise looks me dead in my eyes, as if she has the power to hypnotize me. She touches her fingers to the skin of my arm, just beneath my sleeve, and I am immediately disarmed. I look from her hand back to her eyes.

She leans toward me, and I prepare for her to kiss me again, hoping that I can savor this one even more than the first one, but she only says, in that sweet, sultry voice of hers, "I want my kisses from the Hershey Store in Times Square."

I nod my head. I'm starting to get a craving for some Reese's Peanut Butter Cups, anyway.

I pay the bill, and as soon as I stand up, my head begins to swirl a little. Denise stands up with no problems, her tolerance level clearly much higher than mine.

We walk outside and I stand away from her so that she can hail a cab. When one stops, I walk over and hop in alongside her. This is the way that brothas catch cabs when they are rolling with beautiful women, especially in "lighter" touristy areas at night. If you're with a white person, that person has to hail the cab. If there's no white person with you, you let the lightest skinned person hail the cab (a woman is preferable). And if you are traveling in a band of brown or dark brown, the only option you have in some areas is to let the beautiful brown sister you are with hail the cab. Some of these cab drivers in The City might be some racist, profiling jackasses, but they always stop for a beautiful woman, regardless of shade. That's how we grab this cab coasting down through the Village.

I see the cabdriver sigh when he sees me get in, but he can kiss my ass with that nonsense. As soon as I close the door, Denise tells the cab driver to foot it to the Hershey Store in Times Square, and the car pulls off immediately.

"Damn, this guy is driving fast," I whisper to Denise. "He must not want us to be in the backseat long enough for our asses to leave impressions in the vinyl."

She winks at me and starts to push her ass harder into the seats. "Well my ass will be printed in this seat," she responds, her voice a whisper.

"You are cool-ass people," I say, smiling and pushing my ass deeper into the seat, too.

"You ain't so bad yourself," she says.

I see the cab driver glimpsing us in his rearview mirror. "Everything okay back there?"

"Yeah," I say. "Everything is copacetic!"

Denise starts to laugh, and I begin to wonder if two people have ever been kicked out of a cab for grinding their asses into the backseat.

By the time we pull up to the Hershey Store, I know the cab driver is relieved to get rid of us. I pay him and we walk into the store.

Stuffed chocolate bars and large candy displays surround us, and I realize I could probably eat every single piece of candy in here. Denise heads right for her Kisses, and as she lifts a large bag from the shelf, I have a fleeting thought that we are no closer to figuring out this *Soul Sista* situation than when we started. I don't care anymore though. I'm having fun for a change, and there will be plenty of time to worry later.

"You should come to our open mic poetry event this Friday," I tell her.

"For real. I hope you don't expect me to read anything," she responds.

"You can read if the spirit hits you, but you should come just to enjoy yourself."

She smiles. "So how much is the cover charge?"

"You're my guest, so I got you covered," I respond.

"Oh, Cool, you are *so* becoming my best friend right now," she says. "Close your eyes."

"Why?"

"I'm gonna give you a kiss."

"Ha ha," I respond sarcastically, closing my eyes and holding out my hand to receive one of the pieces of candy she has just picked up.

Her lips press against mine softly and before I know it, I am kissing her back. After a moment she steps back slowly.

"What was that about?" I ask, realizing that she has kissed me twice in one night.

"I don't know, right?" she says. "And to think I was really gonna put some candy in your hand up until the last second."

"You don't hear me complaining, do you?" I say, smiling.

She returns my smile. "We can't do this."

"Do what?" I ask.

"This—whatever you want to call it."

"We're just two friends hanging out," I say.

"Well, we should probably keep it that way—for both of our sakes."

I nod, trying to clear my head. "You're still in-vited to the poetry open mic, though," I say.

Denise smiles. "We'll see," she responds. "But right now I just want to enjoy this chocolate." She waves the bag playfully in my face.

At this moment, I realize that we might actually be far worse off from when we started earlier in the evening. Not only have we failed to find a resolution to our problem, but according to the growing feeling in my gut, we might have actually created a whole new problem to worry about.

25

———

In the safe confines of my bat cave, I stare at the dark ceiling, the earth around me continuing to move slowly, but the monotony of blackness stabilizing me so that the alcohol doesn't do a number on me. I inhale slowly, feeling the cool air of the room move through my nostrils. I am suddenly aware of my lips, and I can still imagine Denise's lips pressed against mine.

I want to kick myself. What the hell am I doing, I think. I must be out of bad ideas so I have to invent new ways of messing up my situation. Couldn't I see any of this coming? I know it wasn't all her. I definitely didn't mind any of the things she did. In fact, I wanted her to do them.

I can still see that amazing smile, her dimples dancing in her cheeks as she looks at me. Her eyes are doe-like beneath her old school glasses, and her reddish-brown Afro puff complements her brown skin in a way that makes me think of chocolate. She really is beautiful, but not in the look-at-me way that a lot of other women try to be. She has a quiet, almost understated, beauty that doesn't really take hold of your imagination until you are apart from her.

I close my eyes, suddenly aware that there is a part of me that, I hesitate to admit, likes her. And this is exactly what I don't need when I have to comb through these other train wreck dates to produce a "winner" for the magazine. For a fleeting moment, I consider if I might be able to choose Denise, but I realize that wouldn't be advisable, given the resources that *Soul Sista* has already invested in this process. Plus, I doubt if Denise is really interested in me in that way. The alcohol was probably more to blame for everything that's happened than anything else. All I've managed to do is confuse the hell out of myself even further.

I walk over to my stereo system and turn on some Slakah the Beatchild and wander back to my bed. The mellow groove quickly envelops the quiet room, and I recast my gaze at the pitch-black ceiling.

As much as I try to ignore my evening with Denise, I find that her smile is there every time I close my eyes. And even more, I find myself unable to suppress my desire to see her again.

❧

BEFORE WE OPEN THE STORE THE FOLLOWING morning, J and I hold one of our semi-monthly meetings. The first thing I ask him is whether or not he's committed to us continuing the business in the way that we've been doing it.

I expect him to take offense to the question, but he only sighs, as he weighs the question.

"At one point I was thinking we could go strictly

virtual with our store and carve out our own little space like Okayplayer.com, but I like being able to walk into a physical store and sell things to our customers, face-to-face. I like seeing people discover new music," he says. "You just can't get that from iTunes. But I'm not gonna lie to you, if it wasn't for business picking up over the last few weeks, I might've toyed with the idea that we should try something else."

I nod. I know he's just being honest. "I really want to see us make this store work," I say. "I didn't even know that I could want to see something succeed as much as I want to see this place succeed."

"I can tell. You've gotten more dates from this business than you can probably stand," J says, laughing.

"I did it for us, though."

"Of course," J says. "I would've done the same thing."

I know J is making light of the situation only because he probably feels differently. The bottom line is that I haven't been here as much as I would've normally, and while I can say it was part of my marketing obligations to the business, I have essentially been in and out of the store on what basically amounts to a series of dates. In any other business, except maybe prostitution, to take off so much time for personal interactions would be tantamount to gross neglect.

"Dude, I just want to thank you for being patient with me. All of this has been more than I expected, and I know I haven't been here all of the time, but I just wanted to let you know that I appreciate you and what you do for us here."

J nods, and I can see in his eyes that my sentimentality has softened him. "Hey, Cool, that's what business partners do. We support each other. And if it hadn't been for you and this *Soul Sista* thing, we might not have gotten that influx of customers over these past few weeks."

I know he is being both generous and modest, but knowing him like I do, I have to let him tell it with his spin.

"So did you ever decide what you were going to do about the situation with *Soul Sista*?" J asks.

"Dude, I don't have a clue the first. If I could have it my way, I'd just pick Denise."

J bucks up. "Denise? The chick who keeps calling here?"

"Yeah, that's the one."

"Can you even do that?"

"Probably not."

"Hold on," J says. "When did you start talking to Denise? You guys went out on a date or something. Inquiring minds want to know. Inquiring minds GOT to know. Fill a brotha in!"

"I don't know. We've met up a few times to discuss all of this blogging stuff."

J's left eyebrow arches. "Aha!" he says authoritatively. "Spending all of that time around her must have sunk into your brain."

"I think I was cool with everything until last night. We went out to discuss whether I still needed to pick someone, and we got a little tipsy and might have kissed," I say.

"Might have?"

"Did," I say. "We *did* kiss."

"How do you go out with someone on business and end up kissing?"

"I don't know. It kind of just happened."

"So now you call yourself liking her, too?" J asks.

I shake my head. "This is different. With the other women I had to work to find out what we had in common, but with Denise, it all just came naturally."

J lowers his head, shaking it as if he can't believe I could make things any more complicated than they already are. "Well, there's only one thing you can do in a situation like this, especially if you have to pick someone."

"What's that?"

"You select the woman you want to build something with."

"Even Denise?"

"Only if you're willing to tell the truth this time."

26

———

After I compose the initial rough draft of my last blog entry, I reread it several times, debating whether or not I should proceed with submitting it. Before I wrote it, I replayed all of the dates I had been on and reread the previously published blog entries. It dawns on me that my selection could've been any of the three women I went out with, if the first dates were any indication. My date with Sarah had gone well. Part of me had even considered calling it a day right then. After all, what was the point in going out on the other dates if I already had someone I could get along with? But then there was my date with Taylor, and she showed equal promise. Frankly, Taylor wasn't the type of woman I had ever really thought I would date, but I felt that there was something there beneath it all, definitely something worth exploring. Even Rochelle had some potential initially, although I don't know how much of that date was really genuine on her end.

But just as quickly as those situations had bubbled with potential, they all popped in my face.

As I finish reviewing this final blog entry for

the umpteenth time, I close my laptop. I don't want to send it out just yet. I still have a day before the deadline, but I already know what I want to say. The only thing I want to do now is see Denise one more time. What she thinks of this is more important to me now than it has ever been before.

&.

IT'S NEARLY FIVE O'CLOCK IN THE EVENING when Denise returns my call. I'm surprised at how nervous I am when I hear her voice. I want to ask her if I crossed her mind today or if she thought about last night as much as I have, but instead I play the cool role, hoping to live up to my name.

"Sorry it's taken me a while to get back to you," she starts.

"That's no problem. I know how it is when things get hectic."

I decide to push on the conversation a little. "I really enjoyed myself last night."

She chuckles under her breath. "I had a good time, too—much better than I should have."

"Don't say that," I respond. "You deserve to have as much fun as you can stand."

"If only it were that simple."

"It really is that simple."

We sit silently on the phone for a few seconds before I start to speak again. "We should get together again."

"And do what?"

I wonder if she is tempting me or distancing herself. "I just want to be around you."

"Awe, isn't that sweet," she says playfully. "I'm not sure that's a good idea though."

"It's funny that you would say that. I've been thinking about last night, and I wanted to talk with you about the connection we made."

She sighs. "I don't think that's such a good idea either."

"We can just get together to talk. I promise we can keep it simple and platonic. I just want to see you again," I say. I hate to plead, but at this point I'm not above it.

"I have to go to an event tonight down near Union Square. I have an extra pass if you want to go with me."

I have to hold my knee down to keep it from bouncing beneath the counter. I want to blurt, "Hell yes, I'll meet you," but I tone it down several notches and just say, "That sounds good."

She gives me the address and time, and I let J know that I have to head out early yet again, but thankfully Ray-Ray is here tonight until closing.

J only offers one note of advice: "Make sure this is the situation you really want to be in, because one night of drinking, in and of itself, does not constitute grounds for a relationship."

I nod, knowing that while he's correct, the butterflies in my stomach are already far ahead of me.

❧

I ARRIVE EARLY TO UNION SQUARE AND DECIDE to wander through Barnes & Noble to occupy myself. Everything reminds me of Denise, though, and I wonder how I came to be captivated with her so quickly. Even as I think back, I realize that I was drawn to her the moment I saw her. I tried to ignore it since we were both pieces of a business transaction, but I don't think I ever really stopped taking notice of her in the subtle ways that one does when he shouldn't be looking at all. Even when I walked out on her at Blockheads, I was kicking myself the moment I did it. But the deal was closed at BBQ's. I wanted to be close to her, to touch her and be touched by her. The first kiss was what summoned the idea that there could possibly be more between us, but the second kiss made me want her in a way that I haven't wanted a woman in quite some time.

I walk to the magazine rack and find myself gravitating toward the latest issue of *Soul Sista* magazine with Janet Jackson on the cover. I flip to the masthead page just so I can see her name in print: Denise Mallory, Lifestyle Editor. My stomach starts to turn flips just looking at it, and I realize that I'm just being damned ridiculous about my infatuation with her.

I sent out my blog entry, which details my growing and ultimate attraction to Denise, moments before I caught a cab down here. I have no idea of whether or not she will have checked her work email before I see her, but if she has, I will at least be in a position to explain why I wrote what I wrote. Part of me thinks that the idea for my entry alone is absurd, because it defies the expectations of the readers in a number of ways, mainly because Denise was not one of their selections and because I've never written a single thing about any of the outings (which can't rightfully be called dates) that I have experienced with her. I figure the worst that could happen is that

Soul Sista will just refuse to publish my blog entry, but at least I will have, from a professional perspective, delivered to them what they requested of me. It's not my fault that what I've written might fall outside of their expectations.

I put the magazine back on its rack and find a seat where I can check my e-mail and mess around with a few apps on my smart phone. After a while, I want to stand and stretch my legs again, so I walk around the bookstore, browsing the spines of books by my favorite authors, ones that I already have in my personal library at the bat cave. After I have walked around each of the four levels, I glance at my watch and see that the time I was supposed to meet Denise is quickly approaching. I take the escalator down to the first floor, thinking to myself that I should've brought flowers with me or something.

I'm only on the corner for about ten minutes before a cab pulls up, dropping her off across the street from me. As she rises from the cab and smooths out her black mini-skirt, I admire her shapely hips and the way the fabric embraces her form. Everything about her is proportioned and perfectly fit. Though I try to push away the thought of being intimate with her, I know that she could love me down in a way that would leave me fantasizing about her hours— maybe days— afterwards.

"Sorry I'm running late," she offers, as she crosses the street.

"Not a problem," I say. "I just got here myself." Reaching in my backpack, I take out a small bag. "I have something for you."

"Really?" She takes the paper bag and opens it. She begins to laugh. "I almost forgot about this," she says, a smile spreading across her face. The twinkle of her smile is like a soft feather being stroked beneath my navel, and I can feel the butterflies fluttering within.

"I told you I was going to give you one. And you said that you would wear it if I did," I say, happy to see her holding up the C&J's Rare Grooves t-shirt and admiring it.

"Pink?" she asks, her voice full of humor. "I look like a pink kind of girl to you?"

"Actually you look like a beautiful woman who could wear pink just as easily as she could any other color."

"Aren't you a smooth talker," she says.

I watch as she puts the t-shirt back in the bag. Secretly I would love to see her in that t-shirt—and nothing else.

"Do I get a hug or anything?" I ask. "After all, I brought you a t-shirt all the way from Harlem."

She laughs and says, "Of course."

She leans in and embraces me, and I hold her, allowing myself to enjoying the soft feel of her chest pressing against me. Before I release her, I lean in to kiss her, but she turns her face giving me a solid cheek.

"Whoa," I respond, feeling as if I got kicked in the chest. "Did I do something wrong? I didn't mean to offend you or anything."

She looks at me as if she is embarrassed by the situation. "I just think we should keep everything professional, you know."

I'm at a loss for words as I consider this, and I wonder if I have done something to upset this delicate balance that we've established. In my mind, I've been cool and nonintrusive, patient, and far from clingy. Suddenly, it dawns on me that she probably hasn't read my email yet.

When I'm finally able to find the words, I say, "Denise, if I did something to rub you the wrong way, please let me know."

"You didn't do anything. Last night was just a bit extra for me."

Please don't blame it on the alcohol, I think to myself.

"I might have had too many drinks and let things go too far," she continues.

Shit.

I reach for anything. "Well, can I ask you a question?"

She looks like she would rather do anything else, but she agrees, probably because she knows that she just dissed me and delivered a bomb to me all within two minutes of our meeting.

"Denise, are you attracted to me?"

"What kind of question is that?"

"Could you please answer that question for me?" I say, trying to steady myself.

"Yes. Of course I am. You are a very attractive man," she responds.

"And do you think that we get along well?"

"Well enough for what?" she says, shifting the burden to me.

"Well enough to spend more time getting to know each other," I say, attempting to sound unfazed.

She shakes her head as if to clear her thoughts. People move around us, and there is a line beginning to form at the door to the club a few yards down the block.

"Cool," she finally says, "what do you want from me?"

I inhale deeply and pace my words. "I want to get to know you better."

"Know me better how?"

"In the way that a man and woman get to know each other when they realize they have chemistry."

She smiles, but not in that affectionate way. She seems increasingly bothered with my line of questions, but I feel like I am unable to let the situation get dismissed so easily. I've always been a person to fight for the things I wanted, and if she's going to shoot me down, I want her to do it in a way that removes all hope from the table so I can try to shake her from my thoughts.

"Cool, you're a nice enough guy, but we can't do this. Maybe my inviting you here tonight wasn't such a good idea."

The sting is so hard that I realize whatever I say to her next will clearly affect not only our evening, but any future involvement we have with each other.

"Okay. But can I say one last thing, and I promise after this I will not bother you with anything else."

She nods.

"I never asked for any of this—these dates or this blog or even this situation of us standing here talking about all of this right now, but I understand that we all make decisions and life just happens in the meantime. I didn't know you would creep into my dreams or that you would find some magical way of knocking me off my feet. And then you kissed me. And I know it's easy to stand back and blame it all on the drinks, but I believe that drinks bring out the truth, not the lies. I know I was intoxicated, but it wasn't off of the liquor. It was off of you. Now I can't shake the thoughts of your lips pressed against mine, the sweet music of your voice, the way you smile. Now all I do is dream about you."

She smiles. "You are so corny."

I can't tell if she is joking or not. Her smile doesn't tell me either way. I wait patiently, hoping for some clarification.

"Every Stevie Wonder song in the book?"

"What?" I ask, confused.

"You just used all of these Stevie Wonder songs to describe me. Am I supposed to be your Stevie Wonder lyric girl?" she asks, her voice still ambiguous.

"I swear I didn't know I was doing that, but now that you mention it, you are my Stevie Wonder lyric. You are my choice."

She lowers her head and looks away. "What if I don't want to be your choice?"

"Then I'll leave you alone and never bother you again. I've already sent you my blog entry, and you are the one I pick. If you want to run it, fine. If not, I will understand. All I want is the chance to get to know you better."

The line at the door continues to move as the club begins admitting people with the proper passes. Denise looks in the direction of the door. I can sense that she is ready to go in, but there is nothing in her look that is inviting me to accompany her.

"I know you've got to go do your job, and I know I just dropped a lot on you just now," I say.

"And I know you probably need some space right now."

Her eyes are piercing, and for the first time, I realize that I have made a huge mistake.

"What gave you the right to write about me? Huh? You were given specific instructions. I even went out on a line for you—repeatedly—this entire time. And this is the way you repay me? By making me some kind of spectacle for my own readers?"

"That's not what I was trying to do," I say. "I just wanted to tell the truth about how I felt."

She looks at me, gnawing slightly on her inner cheek. "Damn, Cool! Is everything about what you want?"

I want to say "no," but I don't think I should say anything. She is more upset than I expected she would be, and frankly, I don't know what to do.

"I've got a job to do now," she says, turning and walking away.

I want to call out after her, but my words, once so sure, betray me. I can only watch her as she heads into the club, alone.

27

Rather than return home, I pick up my phone to check on Angie and to see how her trip to Alabama went. After several rings, she answers, her voice actually more upbeat than I expected it to be.

"Cousin!" I say. "How are you doing?"

"I'm good, Cool. Just trying to get Aaron ready for bed. What are you up to?"

"I had some plans that fell through, and now I'm down just off of Union Square. I figured since we haven't talked since you got back that maybe I could roll through before heading home."

"That's cool. Tracy has been tired from the trip, so she'll probably be out like a light when you get here."

"I understand," I say. "I can be over there in about thirty minutes or so. I think I'm gonna walk. I need to clear my head."

"It's like that? Damn. We definitely need to catch up when you get here."

"So I take it everything went good with Aunt Jonetta."

"We'll have to talk about that one, too."

"Well, okay then," I say, attempting to fight the urge to start inquiring in more detail about her trip.

When I hang up the phone, I cross the street and start heading west. With minimal lighting between the avenues, I find myself walking through the shadows, passing the occasional person who seems more afraid of me and my blackness than the more probable dangers lurking in the alleys between the buildings, things like cat-sized rats and would-be muggers.

With each block I pass, the sting of Denise's diss starts to lighten, but I still wonder what went wrong. Did I come on too strong or did I just come at her the wrong way? Did I misread something last night? Did she not kiss me, too? Did we not laugh and talk and enjoy each other's company? I feel like I'm incapable of reading any kinds of signals at this point.

I come to a light at the intersection of 19th Street and Fifth Avenue, and I wonder what's next for me. I pray that things go well with the poetry reading tomorrow night, and I realize that while my love life is probably of interest to only a handful people at this point, it's become of major interest to me. At this point, I don't even know if any of this has adversely affected our bottom line at the store. Part of me just wants things to go back to the way they were before any of this started. But now something is awakened in me, and I find myself craving the companionship of a woman, the *right* woman. I thought Denise would be that person, but I guess I set myself up to be wrong about that, too.

"Hey, dude," a brother with dreadlocks says as I reach the opposite corner.

I look up, unsure of whether I need to be in defense mode or not.

"The t-shirt!" he says, pointing to my C&J's Rare Grooves shirt. "That place is off the hook! Hold up. Dude, you're that guy from the store, aren't you?"

I nod. "What's up," I say, dapping him and thanking him for being a customer.

"Man, I try to make it up there every month to see what's new."

I try to place the man's face, but I can't really remember him. This is probably the side effect of my persistent absence at the store.

"Have you been following my blog?" I ask.

"What blog?" the guy responds.

"On the *Soul Sista* website."

"That women's magazine? You got something on their website?"

"Well, I used to," I say.

"Ah nah, man. I ain't even catch that. Should I check it out?"

I shake my head. "It's not about the music, so I wouldn't waste time with it."

"Oh, a'ight. Be easy then. I'll probably check you in a few weeks."

"Most definitely," I respond as he walks away.

I stand there, pleasantly surprised. Apparently *Soul Sista's* website doesn't control all of our customer base after all. There are still people out there who simply appreciate our business for what it is, minus all of the rah-rah and hoopla we've managed to drum up over the past few weeks. The guy who just walked away was the kind of customer we went into business for in the first place, and the fact that I didn't recognize him as a loyal customer grates on my nerves just as much, if not more than, Denise's dismissive behavior. Maybe somewhere along the way I've become detached, lost in this maze of life. I want to run after the guy and ask him his name, but I know that that moment has come and gone. I try to remember his face as best I can so when he comes back to the store, I can acknowledge him.

By the time I reach Angie's apartment, I'm in a fairly tranquil state, although the pain and shame of earlier are still lurking somewhere beneath the surface. When Angie answers the door with her customary bear hug, I can tell that she needed to see me just as much as I needed to see her.

"I hope I didn't wake anyone with the buzzer," I say.

"No. Everyone's knocked out, and both of them sleep hard, I'ma tell you," she says, ushering me into the den, where only the light of a lamp next to the couch and the flat screen television are on. I take a seat on the couch, while Angie hits the switch on her favorite La-Z-Boy recliner and gets comfortable.

"So how was the trip to Alabama?" I start.

"You thirsty?" Angie responds, getting up from her chair and walking into the kitchen.

"Sure. What you got?"

"A little orange juice and Tanqueray? That okay?"

"Sure," I respond. Even after all of these years, my cousin's default alcoholic drink of choice is still gin and juice. She was the quintessential Snoop Dogg fan back in the day, and I suspect that old habits die hard.

She returns a few minutes later with the drinks,

and I repeat my question. "How was your trip to Alabama?"

She places her drink on the end table next to the recliner and sits down, pulling the switch as she nestles back against the cushions.

"About as good as you could expect," she says.

I nod and take a sip of the drink. Strong as usual. If it weren't for the orange color, I would think it was straight gin. "Did Aunt Jonetta give you grief while you were there?"

"She was true to form, and I guess I could just take that whatever way it needs to be taken," she responds.

I put the drink down and look at her. "Do I have to keep asking questions, or are you going to tell me what happened?"

Angie takes a long swig, rotating the glass in her hand, as if such a concoction only needs to be rotated a few times to create the perfect balance of citric juice and "kick a hole in your chest" alcohol. When she finally looks up, she says, "You know we drove all the way there, right? All the way down to Birmingham. Damn near took us twenty hours. And it wasn't easy with a baby *and* a wife who was paranoid that everything south of DC posed some kind of KKK threat the family. By the time we finally got there, I was about ready to pass out. So that's the way I was feeling when we finally pulled up in the driveway."

I nod my understanding and take another sip from my glass.

"So when I pull up," she says, "I see Mama walking up to the door. I don't know what I expected—a glow in her face, a smile or something—

but she sees me and looks at me like I'm some kind of Jehovah's Witness standing at her door trying to give her some stuff she don't even want. I'm like, 'Mama, it's me! Angie!' And she opens the door and starts to come down onto the porch, but then she sees Tracy and Aaron and stops in her tracks. I keep on walking toward her though. I want to hold her and see if she remembers what it's like to be hugged by her only daughter. When I finally get to her and wrap my arms around her, the first thing she says is, 'Every time I see you, you look more like a man.' And then she added on, 'You know it's not too late for you to get saved.' Cool, I can't tell you how quick she cut me on that, but I played like I didn't even hear her. I mean, we had just come all that way."

As Angie continues to describe the awkward way in which her mother met her wife and son, my heart goes out to her. I don't know why I thought things would've gone much better for her. When I called Angie earlier, her voice sounded fine, but now it's like just dragging up the memories of her trip requires us to both get buzzed just to put it out there on the table for discussion.

"You know the worst part of it?" she says. "She never even offered for us to come inside. We did all of this nonsense standing out in front of her house like we wasn't a damn bit of nothing."

I can't wrap my mind around Aunt Jonetta doing that, but then again Aunt Jonetta is known for some pretty strict and conservative behavior. But to treat your own daughter and her family that way, especially after such a long drive, is just one of the meanest things that I have ever heard of anyone in our family doing. At that moment, I realize I have no reason to ever communicate with Aunt Jonetta from here on out. Any woman who would treat such a beautiful person like Angie like road kill has no purpose in my life. I down my drink and lean forward, elbows on my knees. "What did you do then?" I ask.

"I told her that this was my family and that I wanted her to meet them. I even hoped that she would see Aaron's cute little face and want to hold him, but she didn't. She just stood there looking at us. All she could say is that she would pray for us that our son would not go to hell with us. At that point, I knew there was nothing else I could say to her. We got back in the car and drove down the street to the gas station. I pulled over to the side and just started crying. I cried so hard I thought my body was gonna break in half. If it hadn't been for Tracy trying to comfort me, I think I might've scared Aaron with all my boo-hooing."

I shake my head, still upset with Aunt Jonetta. "Want me to make you another drink?" I offer.

"Nah. I'm good," she says, placing her empty glass on the end table. "After we left the gas station, we started driving back towards Atlanta. I was just about to get on I-285 to bi-pass the city, but Tracy told me to stay on I-20. We ended up checking into a hotel and going to that new aquarium over there. By the time we walked around for a bit, I started to feel a little better. It's funny how we had to only drive two hours over just to fit in. To Tracy's credit, she saved the weekend. After we left Atlanta, we stopped in Washington and just hung out, hoping we could catch a glimpse of the Obamas, you know?" she says, laughing.

I'm so happy to see her smile, and I want to be relieved along with her, but we're both adults and know that smiling doesn't make your problems magically disappear.

"Well, you sounded cool earlier, and you look okay now."

"I tell you what," she says. "When you drive twenty hours only to make a u-turn on a dime, you can look at it only one of two ways: either you say this is just some pure-dee bullshit or you use it to say at least you did your best so you can move on. I think I'm ready to move on. I did my part. I tried, you know? I was respectful, and I stood there and listened to my mother dog me and my family to our faces. But you know what? I'm gonna be okay. I'm at peace with that. If she wants to reach out to me, the lines of communication are there. But I'm not going back to The Ham. Not unless I *have* to go back, if you catch my drift. Funny thing is that I don't think Mama's gonna change. She might, and that would surprise the hell out of me, but I'm not holding my breath."

I nod. "I feel you." I look at my glass again. "Are you sure you don't want another drink?"

She smiles at me. "Well, I'll fix it, because if I let you make these bad boys you'll put too much orange juice in them." Then as a side note she adds, "You remember that scene from *Harlem Nights*? 'Who drunk up all the orange juice and left just a swallow in the container?' See, what Della didn't know is that I could take that swallow and make a hell of a gin and juice, know what I'm saying?"

We laugh, and it feels good to release.

She walks into the kitchen, and while she

makes the drinks, I look around her apartment. It's actually a nice spot in a nice neighborhood. You can tell that both she and Tracy work hard to make a good home for Aaron. Even the artwork on the walls reflects some degree of consideration. There's nothing in this apartment that looks like it was thrown together as an afterthought. But Aunt Jonetta will never see any of this. She will never know how well her daughter did for herself, and while I know Angie will have to make peace with that, I want so badly to reach into myself and pull out something that could make everything better. I realize that sometimes you just have to let things be as they are and be okay with that. As this realization dawns on me, I understand now that I just have to make peace with my own situations. In fact, I feel strange even thinking about my little hurt feelings in light of the pain my cousin is going through.

When Angie returns with the drinks, she immediately apologizes for not keeping up with my blog. "Did you ever decide which of the women you were going to pick for your blog?"

I feel funny even going into any of this after all that she's told me, but then I remember that my love life is the entertainment for thousands of black women. Why shouldn't my cousin be any different? In fact, I am actually glad that I can help take her mind off of her own problems.

"I did pick someone, but it wasn't anyone that I went on a date with," I say.

"Word? Who did you pick?"

"I don't think so," I say. "I picked this sister named Denise. She's an editor at the magazine."

"*Soul Sista* magazine?" Angie asks, her eyes as large as basketballs.

"Yes," I say, laughing at her expression.

"Talking about flipping the damn script, cousin! Can you even do that?"

"Well, that's what I did, whether they wanted me to or not."

"Does this Denise girl know that you're about to put y'all's business out on Front Street?" Angie asks.

"You want to hear something funny? I just came from seeing her, and when I told her I was feeling her after our last date and that I chose her for this whole deal, she straight shut me down."

Angie takes a sip of her drink, a giant smile on her face. "Please fill me in. Don't leave a sista hanging like this."

As I tell her about the date—or what I am now officially referring to as a date—I walk her through my thought process from beginning to end. "I figure she's the only logical choice. But I suspect she doesn't want to be my choice. I already sent her my entry, so she can do with it whatever she wants to do."

"Just like a man," Angie says.

"What do you mean?"

"You just did all of this stuff without any regard to how she would feel about any of it. You just up and said, 'Me Tarzan. Me like you. Me gon' make you my girl. Unga-bunga.'"

"Unga-bunga?" I say, laughing.

"You know what I mean. See, a woman wants to feel that she has some say-so in things. You kind of made up her mind for her, whether you meant to or not. From what you told me about your date, I know she's feeling you, but you have to be careful when stuff is still brand new. You gotta take it slow."

I consider Angie's words as I take a long swig of my drink. Maybe she's right. Maybe I did treat her like a guy who's become complacent with having women lined up to go out with him. Now I'm feeling like I might have tried too hard to push her into that spot. "What do I do now?"

Angie rubs her sock-covered feet together as she takes another swig. She places her drink down and looks at me squarely. "Let her know that you respect her in all of this and just give her some space. If she wants to have anything to do with you, she knows how to get at you."

"Well, what about my blog entry?" I ask.

"I can't tell you what to do on that one, Cool. You'll have to figure that one out on your own—but I would suggest that whatever you do, you take her out of it. She doesn't need to be a part of this circus masquerading as your love life. You owe her at least that much."

I finish my drink. I can feel a million thoughts swirling around my head, and I know that whatever I decide to do, I need to do it tomorrow and just live with the consequences.

"I guess I should be getting back Uptown," I say, rising from the couch.

"Are we still on for lunch next week?" she asks.

"Most definitely," I respond. "And Angie?"

"Yeah."

"You know that if you and Tracy and Aaron ever need anything, I'm here for you. You guys are my family, and you don't have to drive south of the Mason-Dixon to get at me."

Angie smiles and wraps me in one of her bear hugs, but I can feel every ounce of love in her body coming out through her thick arms. "Love you, cousin," she says.

"I love you, too, Angie. And trust me, I am not the only one who does."

28

When I wake, I sense immediately that this will be a long day. But there's no point in worrying about things outside of my control.

Shortly after I got back home last night, I wrote a new blog entry and saved it before I went to sleep. Now, as I dress for work, I peruse what I wrote and decide to send it to Denise's work e-mail address before I lose my nerve. Once I click send, I close my laptop and go to my closet to pull out one of our store t-shirts, but something stops me. I have a mountain of folded C&J Rare Grooves t-shirts on the top shelf of my closet, but beneath that shelf on hangers that have been barely used in the last few months are my other clothes. Today I reach for those hangers instead and pick out a linen long sleeve button-up shirt and cuff the sleeves to my elbows. I toss on my favorite pair of beat-up jeans and a pair of brown leather business casual shoes that I rarely wear these days, since I tend to favor sleek and colorful sneakers on most weekdays. I wouldn't say that I am dressing outside of my comfort zone today, but I can sense that today is definitely a day for change, and changing my shirt and shoes are the least I can do to sync with my mind.

I arrive at the store a half hour before J comes in. I spend that extra time dusting the shelves and doing last minute tweaks to make sure the furniture is angled properly to accommodate the chairs that we'll put down later this evening. I walk into the back of the store and check the folding chairs that we borrowed from the church down the street and am pleased that everything is in order. I still don't know how many people we will have tonight, but I'm hopeful that the word gets around about the event and that we'll at least get a few of our regular customers to turn out.

By noon I become concerned about the e-mail I sent Denise. I don't know if I really expected to hear back from her about the blog entry, but since I haven't, I'm starting to wonder if she hated my revised entry, too. I stayed up well past midnight writing about how the process of doing these dates has probably taken a toll on everyone. I talked about my failure to make a connection with any of the women selected by the readers, but that I remained optimistic about love. I didn't mention Denise anywhere in the entry, nor did I pass judgment on any of the women I dated. I didn't lament my past relationships or blame anyone for anything. I just wrote my honest feelings and thanked the readers and *Soul Sista* magazine for allowing me the opportunity to reawaken this sense of possibility for my romantic life. The article was not designed to be hot air or fluff, but the honest musings of a brotha turning a certain corner in his life. But all the same, what I wrote was not what *Soul Sista* asked me to write or what Denise spent her time and energy fighting for my right to write. It was simply the truth, not ugly or glamorized.

When Ray-Ray arrives for his afternoon shift, I ask to have a word with him.

"What do you plan on doing with your life?" I ask him.

"Like wife and kids? Crib? That whatchu mean?"

"No. I mean professionally. What do you want to be when you grow up," I say, placing air quotes around the last two words.

"I don't know," he responds. "This is the best job I ever had, and you guys are the coolest people I've ever worked for."

"Are you serious?" I say. "I ride your case every other day."

"I know that you and J ride me 'cause you guys actually give a damn. I'm even thinking about taking some classes at a community college. I mean, and I ain't trying to sound all soft or nothing, but I look up to you guys. You guys went to college and worked on Wall Street and now you all are doing your thing. That's some serious shit, and I got mad respect for you guys. I'm just glad you guys let me even come up in this piece and be a part of all of this."

Now I feel guilty for even telling J several weeks ago about my desire to fire Ray-Ray. "So your dream is to keep working for us?"

"I don't know. Lately I've been thinking about launching a record label or some shit. Maybe drop the kind of music we sell up in here. Before I came to work here, all I listened to was rap, but now I get down with a lot other stuff. Yeah, I still like my Wu-

Tang and shit, but now that I done got that J. Dilla transition into that smoothed-out shit, it's hard to turn my back on it," he says.

I smile. "Well, whatever you decide to do, you have our support. I suspect that you'll be successful at whatever you set your mind to."

"Thanks," he says. Almost as if my words have gotten too personal to him, he changes the topic. "Word on the streets is that we should have a pretty decent turnout tonight."

"Well, that's good news," I say. "You haven't heard anything else about the *Soul Sista* thing, have you?"

"Nah. People are talking about Kanye and that new chick now. Hate to say it, but they done moved on."

"Thank God," I say, wiping imaginary sweat from my brow.

"Yo, it was like that?"

"It's just good to be able to focus on the stuff that really matters. You don't miss normal until everything around you turns crazy."

"I feel you."

By five o'clock, I still haven't heard from Denise, and it starts to dawn on me that things will just be that way and that I should just own my role in it and move on.

J eases up next to me while I'm putting a sign on the door that we will re-open for the open mic in an hour. "I think it's about time to start putting those chairs out."

"Okay," I say, following him to the back of the store and grabbing two chairs under each arm and returning to the front of the store.

"So have you heard from your girl?" J asks.

"Not today. I think that I might've been too extra for her."

"Maybe, maybe not," he says. "In the end it probably has more to do with a lot of other stuff. You've been putting out your true self to people a lot lately, and most people don't operate like that. That's why most new relationships only last about three months. Trust me. I should know. I'm the king of those."

I shake my head, chuckling. "So you're saying I by-passed the 'three month' rule?"

J nods. "You want me to really break this down for you, Cool?"

"Please, my enlightened brother. Break it down so that it will henceforth and forevermore be broke," I joke.

We walk into the back of the store and grab more chairs.

"It all boils down to my theory of B-sides and remixes," he says.

"Oh shit. That again?"

"Just give me a sec to explain."

"Oh, please do, old wise sage," I say sarcastically, although I have been applying his theory since he told me about it nine years ago.

"Imagine admitting on a first date that you're lactose intolerant and that a teaspoon of milk will make you fart your brains out. Or better yet, imagine telling a woman that your supply of In-ternet porn would put to shame anything that your father ever hid around the house. No, these things are the parts we cover up with gentleman-like ges-tures, candlelight dinners, poetry, and love song dedications on radio stations. It would be a turn-off for her to know that you actually spent your Saturday mornings lounging around your apartment in old beat-up boxers eating cereal from a mixing bowl or that the dried skin on your heels could qualify as a lethal weapon in five states.

"But it's not just guys faking the funk. Women have their own dirt, too. Is that really her hair length? Are her breasts really that size? Is she really a fan of my favorite football team? Add to that the real stuff that women would rather keep locked away, and what you have is two people who claim to be getting to know each other without really getting to know each other. Know what I mean?"

"Kind of," I respond. "But what in the hell does any of that have to do with B-sides and remixes?"

"I'm just getting to that part," J says, continuing. "So around that third month, we start to see the B-sides. This is the side that the deejays don't play on the radio. This is the side that is not common knowledge, the side that you don't see from a woman when she passes you on the street or flirts with you at the club. This is the real person starting to come through. The question is whether that B-side is like 'Ode to a Koala Bear,' that forgettable B-side of Michael Jackson and Paul McCartney's 'Say Say Say,' or if the B-Side is an 'Erotic City' to Prince's 'Let's Go Crazy' or a 'La-Di-Da-Di' to Doug E. Fresh and Slick Rick's 'The Show'? In other words, do you like the other side of who she is, that part she doesn't project to the world?

"Add to that the remix component, since people are constantly evolving. Since no two people are static, when you get into a relationship, the relationship can't be static either. So the real question with any relationship is whether the two of you can grow together once you see who the other person really is."

I stare at J for a moment. "Dude, sounds like your theory has evolved a little bit."

J laughs. "Naw, it's the same as it was before. I just didn't give you the whole thing at the time. That would've been like giving candy to a guy who just had three cavities pulled. I had to ration that shit out for you."

"Shiiiiit," I say, laughing.

J shrugs. "All I'm saying is that on these *Soul Sista* dates, you've been skipping over a lot of that A-Side stuff you would've normally rode out back in the day. So now when a woman reacts to you, she's reacting to the post-three month you up front, and for some women, that's a bit much to digest."

"Well," I respond, "I'll have to keep all of this stuff in mind the next time I decide to go and put myself out there again."

By 6:30 we start admitting people, and by seven o'clock the entire store is packed. The microphones on our impromptu stage are hot and ready for action. Even Angie, Tracy, and Aaron are seated near the stage, all of them wearing our store t-shirts.

A list goes around the room and people start signing up in the twenty-five spots we have on the page. Within minutes, the roster is full of poets ready to get up and do their thing.

J gets up and gives an intro for the event, before handing the microphone off to Ray-Ray who agreed at the last minute to emcee for us, when we realized that we hadn't considered how we would handle that part of things. I stand near the back of the store admiring the beautiful throng of people assembled under our roof, and I realize that C&J's Rare Grooves is going to survive after all.

As I watch Ray-Ray turn over the microphone to the first poet, I see a pink shirt out the corner of my eyes. I turn to see Denise walking through the door wearing the shirt I gave her. We make eye contact, and she walks around the crowd toward me.

"You look amazing in that t-shirt," I offer.

"Yeah, I kind of like it—although I'm not really a pink kind of girl," she says, flashing that smile that I love.

I immediately begin to apologize for last night.

"I'm not gonna lie. You put me in a funny space," she says.

"Yeah, I realized that later. I'm sorry about that. I hope my last blog entry didn't get you into too much trouble."

"Actually, my editor-in-chief liked it and wants to run it as-is."

"But what do *you* think?" I ask.

"I think it was, well, you."

I shrug. "Is that a good thing or bad thing?"

"Well, I imagine it's not a bad thing, but you see, I don't really know a lot about you."

"Would you like to get to know me?" I ask.

"Possibly."

"So can I ask you out on another date?"

"Another? We haven't even been out on *one* date," she chuckles.

"Well, I bought you some drinks, some wings, and some candy. In certain small towns in Mississippi that constitutes a date," I say, laughing.

"In New York, we don't consider that a date," she says, batting her eyelashes.

"I would love for you to show me what a real 'New York' date is."

"We'll see," she says, before turning her attention to the stage.

There are a million questions I want to ask her, like "what made her come here?" or "does she forgive me for making a mess of things earlier?" or "will she give me a chance to make all of this up to her?" All I know is that she is here—and that's a good sign. I want to reach out and put my arms around her waist and pull her close to me, but deep down, I know that she will let me know when she wants me to touch her. The ball is in her court, and while I might have bristled at that in the past, I feel okay following her lead.

As I turn my attention away from Denise, I take in the beautiful energy of the room. I look over and see J and Ray-Ray nodding their heads in rhythm with the snaps and claps of the packed room. Even Angie and Tracy look happy, as Aaron lies peacefully between them.

Denise turns to me and smiles, and I feel my spirit lighten. In the back of my mind I know there's still J's theory, but the fact that there's a lot left for Denise and me to learn about each other doesn't seem as daunting as it might've been before.

I find myself visualizing what it would be like to flip the record to Denise's B-Side, and I smile. There could very well be a classic Teddy Riley remix there —and I could definitely get with that.

After all, I've spent my entire life chasing rare grooves.

OTHER BOOKS BY RAN WALKER

B-Sides and Remixes

30 Love

Mojo's Guitar/ (Il était une fois Morris Jones)

Afro Nerd in Love

The Keys of My Soul

The Race of Races

The Illest

Bessie, Bop, or Bach: Collected Stories

Four Floors (with Sabin Prentis)

Black Hand Side: Stories

White Pages

She Lives in My Lap

Reverb: The Adventures of Marz Banx

Work-In-Progress

Daykeeper

Most of My Heroes Don't Appear On No Stamps

Portable Black Magic

ACKNOWLEDGMENTS

As cliché as this might sound, it takes a village to raise a writer, so up front I must thank my parents for putting books into my hands and giving me the confidence to pursue my dreams. Likewise, my brother, Torrey, has provided not only support for this project, but great suggestions to make it into the best manuscript it can be.

Thanks to my writing families from both Callaloo and Hurston-Wright, the wonderful people at the Mississippi Arts Commission, and the following writers who have been very instrumental in my development: Steven Barnes, Aleda Shirley, Tayari Jones, Thomas Glave, Nelly Rosario, Tyehimba Jess, Shonda Buchanan, Michelle Gipson, Victor LaValle, Daniel Black, Colin Channer, Lamar Wilson, Christi Cartwright, DaMaris Hill, Eric Tanyavutti, Aaron Vano, Nancy Garcia, and the awesome Invincible Nine crew. Additional thanks to my colleagues at Lane College and Hampton University and my many students who have often taught me just as much as I have taught them.

To my creative partners Jay Craft, Phill Branch,

Nsayel Mputubwele, Van G. Garrett, and Byron Lee: Thank you! And to the Whittington family: thank you for reading all of the drafts of my books, even the ones that may never see the light of day. Also, thank you, Sabin Duncan, for your endless support of my writing.

A special thank you to Brandon Massey and Zane for taking a chance on me early in my career, and for my dear friend Marie Dutton Brown, who taught me more about publishing than anyone else.

Because I write to music, I have to thank the vast list of soul musicians whose music has often inspired my work, including, but not confined to, the following: Stevie Wonder; Earth, Wind & Fire; Marvin Gaye; Lalah Hathway; Phonte, Nicolay, and the artists of Foreign Exchange Music; Jesse Boykins, III; Georgia Anne Muldrow; Slakah the Beatchild; Maxwell; Raheem Devaughn; Minnie Riperton; and the list goes on and on.

Thanks also to the Walker, Whitmore, Holbrook, and McGee families. Not only am I fortunate to have a great family, both extended and nuclear, I am blessed with a great set of in-laws who have never made me feel like an outlaw. Thanks, Mama Ruth, Edward, and all of the Maxie and Sanders family.

I'd also like to thank my brothers of Phi Beta Sigma Fraternity and my sisters of Zeta Phi Beta Sorority, as well as my AUC (Morehouse, Spelman, Clark Atlanta, Morris Brown) family.

And to all of my friends and family who have supported and encouraged me throughout the years, all the way from West Point, Mississippi, to Harlem,

New York—a list much too long to mention here name-by-name—thank you.

And last, but by no means least, I'd like to thank my much better half, my beautiful wife, Lauren, for standing by me while I worked on various books throughout the years. She has always been my biggest cheerleader, and I could not have done this book without her undying love and support.

ABOUT THE AUTHOR

Ran Walker is a native Mississippian who gave up the practice of law to become a writer. His work has appeared in various anthologies and literary journals, and he was awarded several fellowships, including the Mississippi Arts Commission/National Endowment for the Arts Fellowship for Creative Nonfiction in 2005. He has also participated in both the Hurston-Wright Writers Workshop and the Callaloo Writers Workshop.

Walker serves as a creative writing professor at Hampton University and enjoys spending his time reading, composing music, and exploring the country with his wife and much better half, Lauren, and their little rockstar daughter, Zoë.

He can be reached at www.ranwalker.com.